# Ally Lancaster

## &

## The Gemstone Sirens

## Maci Smithers

5th Corner Media LLC.

Perrysburg, Ohio

Maci Smithers/5th Corner Media LLC.

Book Layout ©2015 BookDesignTemplates.com

Ordering Information:

Quantity sales. Special discounts are available on quantity purchases by corporations, associations, and others. For details, contact:

https://jasonsmithers.com/contact

Ally Lancaster & The Gemstone Sirens/ Maci Smithers. —1st ed.

ISBN 979-8-9897033-0-2

# Contents

For Grammy.
Thank you for always supporting me.

You're awesome.

*"One may seem like a gem on the outside…but that doesn't change anything on the inside…"*

# CHAPTER ONE

# Aristar's Birthday

ALLY LANCASTER WOKE UP ON A SATURDAY MORNING. It was really early, but there was no way she could sleep any longer—today was a big day.

Ally got out of bed, slid her feet into her furry gray slippers, and changed the countdown on her desk so that it read '1 Day Remaining.' She glanced over at the maroon-colored dog bed in the corner of her room— empty. Aristar must have gone downstairs already.

She walked downstairs to discover that, as usual, she was the only one awake—except for their two dogs, Rocket and Aristar, who were both scratching at the back door to go outside.

Rocket was a large, slobbery pit bull whose favorite hobby was sleeping. He hadn't touched a toy since he was a puppy. Ally wasn't sure he had even played with one back then.

Aristar, on the other hand, wasn't the *family* dog, really. He belonged just to Ally. He was a massive, fluffy black Labrador—over twice Rocket's size—with pointy, folded ears and a pair of five-foot-long wings. The previous year, Ally had flown Aristar to her school, Willow Reins.

Every time she looked at Aristar, all the memories came flooding back to Ally. They reminded her of how badly she wanted to be back at Willow Reins, the one-and-only school of dueling.

It was where every student was taught how to fight. However, Ally and her friends didn't exactly get to enjoy a full year there like all the other students. They had been at a mysterious castle in the woods called the Enchanted Fortress, which was being possessed by an evil force. The evil force—Zortavka—had been using the Fortress to make terrible things happen at Willow Reins. Ally and her friends had ventured into the wilderness to find the Fortress and defeat Zortavka. They had scared her away from the Fortress, but there was no guarantee that she was gone for good.

Ally hoped that her second year would be just as exciting as the last, with an equal amount of action-packed fighting and exhilarating adventure.

There was only one day until Ally and Aristar's next flight to Willow Reins, and Ally was getting tired of summer vacation. She was as ready as ever for this flight.

Tomorrow was probably the most important day of the summer for Ally. Not only was it the day of the flight to school, but tomorrow was Aristar's birthday. He was one of Ally's best friends, so she wanted to do something special for him. The problem was, she wasn't exactly sure what that would be yet.

Ally thought of ideas as she scarfed down her lunch. *I could get him a new toy… no, too simple… I could get him his own house… nope, WAY too expensive… I could throw him a surprise party…?*

Yes, that was it! There would be streamers, balloons, cake for dogs (Ally had no idea how she was going to find one of those but was determined to find a way), and more—the whole thing sounded perfect for Aristar! Ally would need a whole day to plan Aristar's epic surprise party, and she'd have to get started soon. And since it was a *surprise* party, she couldn't let Aristar figure out what she was up to—he was a lot smarter than most regular dogs, and he definitely could. It would be difficult, but Ally was determined to pull it off.

*Step one: make sure I'm allowed to throw a humongous party,* thought Ally as she finished off her sandwich. The only way to do this step was to ask her parents, who were in the kitchen.

So, like a ninja, Ally crept into the kitchen, trying not to attract the attention of Aristar, who was napping peacefully in the dining room. Her parents were making lunch for her baby sister Amber.

"Mom! Dad! Can I throw a party for Aristar?" She blurted immediately.

"I suppose you could, but you would have to buy everything with your own money," her mom replied.

"Ok, sure!" said Ally brightly. She dashed upstairs to her room, grabbed a sheet of notebook paper along with her set of pens from her dresser drawer, and sat down at her desk. She scrawled down a list of things she would need for the party:

## _Aristar's Epic Party_

_Streamers, confetti, decorations like that_

_Doggy Cake (hopefully DogDaze carries that)_

_A gift (something like a gigantic ball)_

_A good location to throw the party_

Ally folded up the list and stuffed it in her pocket along with all of her allowance from the past couple of months—which, altogether, added up to about $50.

The next step was to go to DogDaze (the pet supplies store just outside of Ally's neighborhood), and get everything. But first, she would need a way to get there.

Aristar was usually her go-to mode of transportation, but since the surprise party was for him, that option was off the table. Her parents had their hands full taking care of Amber, so they couldn't drive her there. Neither could her older sister Ari, for she was at the library studying. Too bad none of Ally's friends lived nearby; last year, when Aristar wasn't available, she would simply hitch a ride on one of their pets. The only other option that she could think of was riding her bike there.

Ally walked out into the garage, where her bright red bike stood balanced on its kickstand. She tied her light blond hair into a long ponytail, put on her helmet, and began riding down the sidewalk to the pet store.

Soon, Ally arrived at DogDaze. She pulled out her list. The first things she needed to get were the decorations.

*Decorations… decorations… where would the decorations be??* Ally thought as she scanned each aisle. She spotted a box on the top shelf of one aisle labeled Puppy Party Package. This was exactly what she needed, as it contained dog-themed balloons, streamers, and lots of other party decorations.

Ally grabbed that and headed down the dog toys aisle. A stuffed squirrel dog toy caught her eye, and she thought it would be a great gift for Aristar, who enjoyed barking at squirrels.

Lastly, Ally had to find a cake. Luckily, there was a section of the store called the Barkin' Bakery. Ally picked out a dog-food-flavored cake with peanut butter frosting. She paid for everything, spending about $35 of her allowance. She planned on using the remaining $15 to get some dog treats as party favors—but later on when her arms weren't full of other things for the party.

Ally mounted her bike. *I did not think this through,* she thought as she attempted to position herself in a way where she could balance the bike and keep from dropping everything—especially the cake. That could smash very easily, and Ally didn't want to have to buy a new one.

With the shopping bags hanging from the handlebars of her bike and Ally holding the cake in one arm, she slowly began riding down the sidewalk.

*This isn't so bad,* she thought, glancing at the cake. Aristar would love it. But taking her focus off of the path in front of her was a poor choice. "Whoa!" Ally yelled as she lost her balance, veering off the sidewalk and crashing into a stop sign. She and the decorations were unharmed, but the cake was completely smashed.

Ally had no choice but to return to DogDaze and purchase a new one. One cake cost $5, and Ally wouldn't have very much to spend on party favors. But the cake was more important.

Soon, Ally got back on her bike, a brand-new, un-smashed cake in her hands. She was going to take the same approach to getting the cake home safely, just this time she would pay full attention to where she was going.

Ally began pedaling and single-handedly steering the bike, eyes glued to the sidewalk in front of her.

Maybe she paid a bit too much attention to where she was going and not enough to the cake, because it slipped out of her hands and splattered on the sidewalk. "Oh, come *on!*" Ally groaned, tossing her head back in frustration. She turned around and headed back to DogDaze.

The sun was beginning to set, and DogDaze was going to close soon. *If this doesn't work, I'm baking the cake myself,* Ally thought, marching back into the store and buying yet a third dog cake. When she walked back through the dog toys aisle, she spotted the toy ropes and an idea came to her.

So, Ally bought a few long toy ropes and used them to tie the cake down to her arm. She rode away from DogDaze.

She made it home, disappointed that she had had to spend the remainder of her money on cake and toy ropes, but at the same time relieved that she had decorations and a cake that was fully intact.

Ally zipped upstairs to her room, set the cake and decorations down on her dresser, and sat down at her desk again. She pulled her list out of her pocket and crossed out everything that she had completed.

<u>*Aristar's Epic Party*</u>

~~*Streamers, confetti, decorations like that*~~

~~*Doggy cake (hopefully DogDaze carries that)*~~

~~*A gift (something like a gigantic ball)*~~

*A good location to throw the party*

There was just one thing that she hadn't completed, and that was finding somewhere for the party to take place. *Where would be a good place to throw a party for a dog...?*

Ally looked around her room for ideas. Her gaze fell upon the window, and she saw Aristar and Rocket outside in the backyard, playing tug-of-war. Well, Aristar was trying to play tug-of-war with Rocket—But Rocket had other plans.

The backyard was the *perfect* spot to throw the party. There was so much room, and outside was Aristar's favorite place to be. Why hadn't she thought of this before?

"Ally! Time for dinner!" Her parents called from the dining room downstairs. She wanted to work on planning the party more and start setting up outside, but it would have to wait. Ally went downstairs for dinner.

Ally finished her tuna casserole in a matter of minutes and then bolted back upstairs.

"Where are you going?" Ari called after her.

"To bed!" Ally replied shortly. She had to wake up early tomorrow morning to beat Aristar outside and set up the party decorations.

And so she went to bed, happily aware that this was the last night sleeping in her own bed. Because tomorrow, she would be at Willow Reins—her favorite place on earth.

## CHAPTER TWO

# Flight of the Slobbery Pit Bull

THE NEXT DAY, AFTER WAKING UP AT 5 AM, Ally skipped breakfast and went straight out to the backyard to begin setting up the party.

She grabbed a couple of fold-up tables from the garage and hauled them out to the backyard. Ally then covered them with the pawprint tablecloths that came in the Puppy Party Package. After that, she hung streamers from the string party lights that surrounded the patio. She blew up a bunch of balloons and secured those balloons to the ground after learning the hard way what would happen if she didn't. And finally, she cautiously placed the cake on one of the tables. After that, her work was done.

***

That night, after a long day of making sure Aristar didn't notice any of the party decorations, Ally found herself outside with her family, waiting for the party to begin.

Ally would be flying to Willow Reins overnight this time around, so she knew she could wait until just the right time to surprise Aristar. It was about eight o'clock. The night air was slightly chilly, and the sky was a dark navy color and flecked with luminescent stars. The moon loomed large, glowing brighter than anything else in sight.

"Okay, I think it's about time to call Aristar out here," said Ally excitedly. She reached into the pocket of her sweatshirt and pulled out a button—the one that was used to summon dueling pets to their owners—and pressed it. She turned to the back door, and as expected, Aristar had appeared on the other side of it, tilting his furry head.

Grinning, Ally slid the door open, releasing Aristar from the house. He trotted outside as if it were a normal night and he was just going outside to do his business. But he stopped in his tracks after taking one look around the backyard.

"Happy birthday, Aristar!" Ally yelled. She was the only one yelling, but she didn't care.

Aristar's collar flew off his neck, shooting into the sky and exploding into fireworks. It flew back, turning back into a collar, and a note slipped out of it. All that was on the note was about fifty exclamation marks.

The party went by fairly quickly; Aristar and Rocket enjoyed their doggy cake, Ally gave Aristar his gift, and then Aristar served Ally and her family a cake that was made for humans.

As they finished their cake, Ally's mom spoke up. "Ally, Ari, are you all ready to head to school in a little bit?"

"Definitely," said Ally. "Wait. Did you just say *Ari*?"

Her dad sighed. "Ari, you *still* haven't told her?"

Ally turned to her sister, who plastered an innocent smile across her face. "What do you mean? Tell her *what*…?" she played dumb.

Their parents gave her a stern look. "You know what."

"What? What is it?" Ally asked frantically. She hated having no idea what Ari was hiding—especially since it involved her.

Ari took a big breath. "Fine. I go to Willow Reins."

Ally's jaw dropped. She had so many questions. "Why didn't you tell me before? How long have you gone to Willow Reins? Who is your dueling pet? How…?"

"I hadn't told you before because I couldn't," Ari explained. "It's because of this magical spell—the Disguise Spell. Principal Washiarota puts it on every dueling pet. It makes it so that Dueling Pets appear as regular animals until the person knows about them. He put it on Rocket, and it's been fooling you up until now since you haven't known that I attend Willow Reins, or that he's my dueling pet. Try looking closely at Rocket, now that you know."

Ally looked at Rocket. She was expecting to see the lazy pit bull that she had known almost all her life, but she was wrong. Rocket now had a pair of majestic, snow-white wings, and a magical collar identical to Aristar's.

Ally was still confused. "Wait. But when I first met Aristar, I had never known that Willow Reins or dueling or magic, or anything like that existed. But I could still see that he had wings and a magical collar, and so could everyone else. Didn't he have that spell thing put on him yet?"

"No," Ari replied. "It's put on everyone's pets as soon as they walk through the doors of Willow Reins."

Ally processed this whole thing for a few minutes. Her shock was soon replaced by anger. "You had *all summer* to tell me. So why didn't you?"

"I just didn't want to, so I didn't," Ari said defensively, raising an eyebrow. "Just be glad I told you at all."

Ally opened her mouth to argue but paused when she heard a faint sound in the distance.

"Does anyone else hear that?" she asked.

"Hear what?" her dad questioned.

It sounded almost like some kind of song, but not a normal one. Someone was singing, but without words.

The mysterious song echoed around the neighborhood. Ally rose out of her seat and began cautiously walking in the direction of the song—which was hard because it seemed to be coming from every direction.

The song was so mesmerizing—hypnotic, even. Ally began to feel weird…like a prisoner held captive by the melody. This song, whatever it was, whoever was singing it, wherever it was coming from, had Ally in a trance.

She couldn't think straight. It was like the singer was luring her toward them with this hypnotic song—and it was working.

Ally forgot where she was. What she was doing. Why she was doing it. She even forgot who she was.

The faint sound of someone calling her name cut through the hypnotizing effects of this song. It grew louder and louder until it caused her to snap out of it.

"Ally!" Ari called. Ally came to her senses and found herself inches away from crashing into the fence of their backyard. "Where are you going?"

"Didn't you hear that…?" Ally thought about trying to convince them that she wasn't joking, but decided against it. "Nevermind. I was going nowhere."

Ally returned to the patio, both confused and concerned by that strange song. But the sound of both Aristar's and Rocket's collars vibrating turned her thoughts to something else. A note popped out of Aristar's collar, and Ally read it.

### Time to take flight! Are you ready?

"Yes!" Ally yelled. She glanced at her watch, and it was nine o'clock exactly. This meant that she would be arriving at about three o'clock in the morning for the celebratory first-day feast.

Aristar got his wings ready and let Ally climb on. Out of the corner of her eye, she saw Ari mount Rocket. She couldn't figure out *why,* exactly, but seeing her sister atop a dueling pet made her angry.

Aristar spread his wings and they took flight.

"Have a good school year!" her parents called after her.

Soon, Ally and Ari were soaring high above the clouds. Ally felt the wind smacking her face. Suddenly, a note and a pen slipped out of Aristar's collar.

*Fast,        Medium,        Slow?*

Ally circled 'fast', and Aristar sped up. A few feet away, Rocket mirrored this action.

"Aristar, bring me to Ari and Rocket," Ally muttered. Aristar veered to the side, and he matched Rocket's pace.

"I still can't believe you didn't tell me," Ally barked.

"It's not my fault, just *let go of it,* ok?" Ari hissed.

*"Let go of it??* I deserved to know and you never told me!"

Ari sighed heavily. "This is my seventh and final year at Willow Reins. *Don't* ruin it for me."

Ally opened her mouth to protest, but Principal Washiarota's calm voice came on over the speaker of Aristar's collar.

"Hello, Willow Reins second-year students! I am speaking to every one of you who are now in your second year. I hope that you all had a stupendous summer, but it's time to return to school, and I hope that that excites you as much as it does me! Let's see… Most of you from last year will be returning, but there are quite a few new students! Your dueling pet will provide you with a slip of paper asking whether you'd like to hear the list of new and returning students."

Ally wrote **Yes.**

"Okay, most of you said 'yes', so here is the list:

Allison Lancaster

Aryanna Parks

Bradley Equere

Cyrus Sticio

Desi Roalire

Emerald Trivala

Emily Rosegold

Gabriel Wouldsar

Harley Latinato

Isabelle Opaline

Josie Encame

Levi Xiax

Lydia Whysperia

Mike Lavacis

Mokona Ami

Nova Thres

Opal Ferary

Quierira Reaerez

Ruby Trivala

Rayna Welner

Sasha Marigold

Trevor Wedfeler

Uranus McFite

Vorlo Wehs

Wildo Waze

Xander Serty

Zerner Turner."

Ally could hear a similar message playing on Rocket's collar, except it was altered to explain information to the seventh-year students instead of the second-years. A minute later, the collar came on again.

"Three of them appear to have the same last name! Siblings, I presume? Anyhow, once you land (which will be in about 5 hours and 30 minutes), you will wait near the entrance for all of your classmates to arrive, then you will all be welcomed inside for the first-day feast. I'll save the rest for when you get here. The sky is dark, so fly safely and be on your guard for airborne monsters. We await your arrival," said Principal Washiarota.

A circular tray came out of Aristar's collar. Around the edges were the ingredients to make s'mores. In the center, a small fire ignited.

Ally was in the process of roasting a marshmallow when Ari spoke again. "Why are you still flying right next to me?"

"We're going to the same place," Ally sighed. She had had enough of this.

"Doesn't mean we have to take the same route," Ari smirked.

Fortunately, Principal Washiarota spoke again.

"Oh! I almost forgot. If you are to run into a problem of any kind, most of you know the drill, but I will repeat it for new students. If you run into problems such as being attacked by monsters, collars not working, getting winded, needing to use the restroom, getting cold or hot, choking on sweets, or pets sending swear notes, don't be afraid to hit the red button on your pet's collar. It will summon the Problem Station, run by Sir Rewndo. Enjoy the rest of your flight." The speaker went silent.

"Anyways, we *do* need to take the same route because our pets are in control," Ally argued.

"That doesn't mean—ugh, never mind!" Ari growled in frustration. "You know what? I might just call the Problem Station on you because you are such a problem!"

"No you won't," Ally said slyly.

"Oh,                                        yeah?"

To Ally's surprise, Ari mashed the red button on Rocket's collar. Both Rocket and Aristar froze in midair, and gray bricks materialized all around them. A familiar-looking, tall, thin man appeared, standing on a brick.

"Heyo again, A'y and A'i Lancaster! Wha' c'n Sir Rewndo do fer ya t'day?" Sir Rewndo beamed.

"My sister is being annoying," Ari huffed instantly.

"What!? You started this whole thing."

"You're    the    only    one    being    annoying."

"No, you are!"

"Absolutely not!"

Sir Rewndo glanced between the two of them, looking lost for words. "Er… I dunno i' thi' coun's as a real prob'em," he said, sounding confused. "Bu' an'way, here's a s'lution! Take two differen' rou'es! Just lemme grab a map…" He returned with a map and spread it out in front of the pets' faces. He traced two different lines. "Rocke' take thi' path, an' Arist'r take this path! Easy peasy!"

"Ok, thanks!" said Ally, glaring at Ari.

"C'ya!"

The Problem Station dematerialized, and Aristar unfroze and turned in a different direction. He continued gliding that way, and Ally finished making her s'more. She bit into it.

"This is amazing," she said through a mouthful of s'more.

Now that she didn't have Ari to worry about anymore, things were going smoothly. The rest of the ride was fast and uneventful; Ally stuffed her face with sweets—which included her personal favorite, Wilma Werrybott's Chocolate Shields—her trusty sword and shield were returned to her, and she read a book about common monsters.

Later, Ally had a countdown clock pulled up on Aristar's collar. She soon found herself counting down along with it. "Ten, nine, eight, seven, six, five, four, three, two, one… ZERO!"

Ally looked down with a smile. She had arrived.

## CHAPTER THREE

# New Acquaintances

ARISTAR LANDED ON THE MOONLIT BRICK WALKWAY THAT LED TO THE ENTRANCE OF WILLOW REINS.

Ally got off and looked around. She spotted the crowd of second-year students, took Aristar's leash, and strolled over there.

Ally scanned the small group of second-years, searching for her friends. She spotted the bench where she had first met one of her friends last year. And sitting on that bench, reading a book titled Good as Gold and accompanied by a giant, white, winged rabbit was one of her best friends from last year—Lydia Whysperia.

"Lydia!" Ally called.

Lydia glanced at her and did a double take. She put down her book and ran over to Ally.

Lydia had ocean-blue eyes and long, dark hair. Ally noticed a faint scar on her arm where she had been bitten by a vampire in the Enchanted Fortress last year.

"Ally!" Lydia exclaimed. "How was your summer?"

"Uneventful," Ally replied with a shrug. She debated telling Lydia about the strange song she had heard after Aristar's party but decided not to. That would have been way too much stress for the first day back at Willow Reins. "How was yours?"

"Also uneventful, especially if you compare it to last year," said Lydia. "Anyway, any sign of Mike or Cyrus yet?"

"Not yet, they must be late," Ally said.

There was a slow creaking sound coming from the entrance of the school. Principal Washiarota, wearing a long, vivid green robe, stepped out onto the stairs.

"Welcome back, second-years," he said. "Most of you already know that I am Principal Washiarota, but for those of you new students, that is my name. We are thrilled to see that you all have made it here safely. But since it is nighttime and monsters come out at night, why don't we head inside?"

Ally and Lydia followed the crowd of second-years into the cafeteria. They lined their pets up against the wall and sat at the same table that they had for every meal (although there weren't many) last year.

"We're ecstatic to see that all of you second-years have made it here safely," announced Principal Washiarota. "Allow me to reintroduce my lovely assistant and wife, Queen Niegro." He gestured to Queen Niegro standing beside him. "Dorm arrangements will be the same as last year, and so will uniforms—as a reminder, girls will wear plaid skirts and proper shirts, boys will wear suits. Enjoy your very late dinner."

At that, everyone began talking loudly.

"I wonder—" Lydia began, but she was interrupted by the by the deafening trumpet of an elephant right behind Ally's head.

Startled, Ally sprung out of her chair and whirled around. Standing in front of her was an enormous, winged elephant—this was unmistakably Ediz, the dueling elephant that belonged to Ally's friend Cyrus Sticio.

Ally turned back around and realized that sitting across from her and Lydia were Cyrus and their other friend, Mike Lavacis.

"Ediz," Cyrus groaned, smacking himself in the face. Mike, meanwhile, had fallen to the floor laughing.

Cyrus had red hair and green eyes, and Mike had brown hair and bluish-gray eyes. Mike's dueling pet was Biggie the Irish Wolfhound, who was lined up against the wall next to Aristar and Wiggles (Lydia's dueling rabbit). Ediz was stomping over there as well.

"Wha—? When did you two get here?" Ally asked frantically, still shaken from Ediz's sneak attack.

"Just a minute ago," said Mike, getting up from the floor and sitting back down.

Washiarota continued speaking. "I know it was inconvenient having to fly in this late at night, so I do apologize for that. When you're finished with dinner, don't forget to stop over here and pick up your room keys before heading to your dormitories. That's all for now; enjoy your dinner."

The cafeteria erupted into noisy chatter.

"So, when—" Ally began, but she was interrupted by a loud slam. Someone had slammed their dinner tray on the table.

Ally turned to face the tray slammer. It was a girl with long brown hair and storm-gray eyes. She was flanked by two other girls who had the same face and stone-cold eyes, except one had blond hair and the other had black hair.

"Could we sit here, by any chance?" the one in the center asked.

"Er—sure," Ally replied. The three girls took their seats at the table. Ally gazed around the cafeteria—there were plenty of open tables, which made her wonder why these girls chose this one.

"Wait, are you the three new sisters?" Lydia questioned.

"Yes," the brown-haired one replied quickly. "I'm Ruby. These are my sisters: Emerald…" she gestured to the blond-haired one "…and Sapphire." She gestured to the black-haired one.

"Welcome to Willow Reins!" Ally exclaimed through a mouthful of couscous.

"Thank you," said Sapphire.

There was silence for a few moments. Nobody seemed to want to be the first to talk to or question these new girls. Whatever it was, whether it was good or bad, Ally was certain she wasn't the only one who detected something strange about them.

Tired of this awkward silence, Ally was the first to speak. "So… what dueling pets brought you three here?"

All three of them looked clueless as if they had no clue what a dueling pet was.

"You know…the winged pet that brought you here?" Ally elaborated.

In unison, they all replied immediately.

"Donkey," said Ruby.

"Unicorn," said Emerald.

"Werewolf," said Sapphire.

"Both of them are confused; a donkey brought us all here," said Ruby. Her sisters both nodded vigorously.

"Wait. You mean one single donkey took all three of you here?" Mike interrogated. "You didn't all get your own pets?"

"Yes," said Emerald firmly.

Cyrus scanned all of the second-years' pets lined up against the wall. "That's weird. I don't see any donkeys."

"Oh! Er, she means a chameleon. A chameleon totally brought us here," Sapphire corrected quickly after spotting a chameleon lined up along the wall.

"'Donkey' and 'chameleon' are easy to confuse. They sound so alike, right??" Emerald giggled nervously.

"Nope, not at all," blurted Mike before Ally had the chance to jump in and say something else.

"He means yes, they sound so similar," Lydia lied, catching on to Ally's strategy.

Before long, students were beginning to finish up their dinners and file out of the cafeteria. Ally figured she should probably do the same, but she wanted to interrogate the triplets more.

"Have you three gotten your dorm number yet?" Ally asked.

"We'll be taking room F on floor 73," said Ruby.

"That's right next door to ours," Lydia commented, glancing uneasily at Ally.

"When did you talk to Washiarota about that? I thought you'd been sitting here the whole time," said Ally.

"Oh, we didn't ask him, we just decided that would be our room," replied Sapphire.

"But you have to ask, you can't just randomly decide you want that room," said Mike.

"We do what we want and don't need anyone else to tell us what to do," Emerald snapped. It could have just been the lighting, but Ally could've sworn she saw Emerald's eyes flash bright green.

"Well, it was nice meeting you four, but we should be going to our dorm room now," said Ruby. "Bye!"

"'Bye…" Ally's voice trailed off as the triplets left the cafeteria together. She turned to her friends.

"Does anyone else think there's something… off about those girls?" she asked once the triplets were out of earshot.

"Definitely," replied Lydia.

"Uh-huh," said Mike.

But Cyrus didn't respond. He was too busy watching the only chameleon in the room being led out by another student.

At around four o'clock, everyone finished their dinner. Ally and Lydia picked up their room keys from Washiarota and started heading to the girls' dormitories with Aristar and Wiggles. They walked through the lobby and to the elevator with the pink sword painted on it.

Once they got in, Ally pressed the button for Floor 73. The doors slid open, and they strolled down the carpeted corridor and found Room E. Ally scanned her keycard on the door, and the two of them stepped inside.

The room was just as stunning as Ally had remembered it; there were two white canopy beds with soft linen bedding, string lights strung across the entire room, a bathroom, a snow-white beanbag chair in the corner, a huge walk-in closet, a balcony, and a makeup table (that was the only part of the room that Ally would never use).

Ally's and Lydia's school uniforms were neatly folded on their beds, right next to their armbands and a gift.

Ally darted over to her bed, strapped on her armband, and opened her gift. Inside was a badge that read Willow Reins Second-Year, a card from Washiarota, and a teddy bear that said I Heart Willow Reins.

Before long, Ally changed into her pajamas and went to bed, Aristar curled up at her feet. She fell asleep in a matter of seconds with nothing on her mind but how glad she was to be back.

## CHAPTER FOUR

# The Song of the Night

EARLY THE NEXT MORNING, ALLY CHANGED INTO HER UNIFORM AND HEADED BACK DOWN TO THE CAFETERIA FOR BREAKFAST. They were serving chocolate chip pancakes and sausage, just like they did for the first breakfast of every year. Ally met up with her friends at their usual table. But to Ally's dismay, the triplets were also there.

"Oh…hi again," said Ally, plastering a fake smile across her face.

"Hello," replied Ruby calmly. "Nice day, isn't it?"

"Certainly," Ally replied through gritted teeth.

Luckily, she didn't have to make conversation with them for very long, because Sir Rewndo disco-danced his way over to their table, whistling.

"'Ello, A'y, 'Dia, 'Ike and Cy'us!" he exclaimed. "An' a few new studen's! Hmm… ya mus' be the Tr'valas, R'by, Em'rald, and Sapp'ire!"

"Uh-huh," said Emerald, giving Rewndo a distasteful look. Suddenly, Aristar, Wiggles, Biggie, and Ediz darted over to Ally, Lydia, Mike and Cyrus.

"What's going on?" asked Sapphire.

"Well, since ya three are new, lemme exp'ain the Sunl'ght Send!" said Rewndo. "I's wh're ya send people mail, or people send ya mail through yer pets' collars! I'ma show yeh how it works!"

He pulled a blank piece of paper out of nowhere and scribbled a little message on it. "Oy! Duggies! C'mere!" he called to Aristar and Biggie. Both dogs came scampering over. "So, first, yeh say who ya wanna send it teh. A'y Lancaster," he ordered. He inserted the piece of paper into a slot on Biggie's collar, and it slid out of an identical slot on Aristar's collar.

"Um…cool," said Ruby.

"Oy! I gotta get to class! C'ya!" Rewndo exclaimed, checking the clock. He disappeared into thin air.

"Students, please report to your first class, Protection Skills," Queen Niegro instructed.

Lydia was on her feet and speed walking out of the cafeteria before Queen Niegro even finished speaking. Ally, Mike and Cyrus followed her.

The four of them were just leaving the room when Ally was caught in the doorway by a girl with waist-length blond hair, who was dragging a tiny chihuahua on a bright pink leash. It was none other than her worst enemy from last year—Aryanna Parks.

"Well, well, well—the hideous beast returns," Aryanna smirked.

"Yeah, you. You are the random hideous beast who is sadly returning," Ally blabbed. She tried to walk past but was blocked by Aryanna.

"Ha-ha. As if," Aryanna scoffed, rolling her eyes. Her eyes were drawn over to Aristar, who was innocently standing beside Ally, and she leaped backward. "Ew! Get your mangy mutt away from my designer dress!"

Ally didn't have time to deal with her. "Get out of the way, Aryanna, I'm trying to get to class," she growled, pushing past Aryanna and heading off towards the dueling fields.

"Listen up, students!" said Madame Miles once everyone arrived. "You all know the basics of dueling, so I'll call you 'amateurs,' alright? After this year, you may just be considered skilled duelers! Now let's begin."

"Today we'll practice shield parries. With a successful parry, your opponent will likely drop their weapon and therefore be wide open for you to strike. Go on, choose your partners."

Ally started towards Lydia, but Ruby stopped her in her tracks. "We're partners," she decided firmly.

"Oh, well, okay," said Ally with another fake smile. She didn't want to be partners with Ruby, but didn't want to mess with her.

Ally looked over her shoulder and saw that Lydia had become partners with Sapphire, and Mike and Cyrus had ended up in a group of three with Emerald. For whatever reason, these new girls seemed to really like Ally and her friends.

"Zerner, Rayna, you two will be my examples. Rayna, take out your shield, Zerner, sword."

The two of them did as told.

"Zerner, try and hit Rayna, and Rayna, use your shield to block the sword."

Zerner swung the sword, and Rayna whipped her shield out in front of her to block it. The sword went flying out of Zerner's hands and across the field.

Ally turned to Ruby. "Do you want to do the sword or the shield?"

"Shield," said Ruby.

Ally pulled out her sword, expecting Ruby to get her shield, but she didn't.

"I don't have a shield," said Ruby. "Or a sword."

"Um… okay… you can use mine, then…?" Ally said questionably. Not having dueling pets was one thing, but having no weapons was a whole different level. You couldn't really be a dueler without a sword. But still, Ally kept quiet and handed over her shield.

Ally and Ruby practiced the moves and the rest of the class passed uneventfully. Before long, the class was strolling to Sir Rewndo's garden for Pet Care.

"Ruby didn't even have a sword or shield," Ally muttered to her friends as they walked.

"Neither did Emerald," said Cyrus.

"Sapphire didn't, either," Lydia added.

"I'm starting to think they don't belong here," said Mike, eyeing the triplets skeptically.

This thought hadn't yet crossed Ally's mind. The more she thought about it, the more it made sense. If they didn't have dueling pets, how did they receive their letters of acceptance to Willow Reins? How did they get there? Why didn't they get weapons? But still. The doors of Willow Reins were heavily guarded and protected, so that not just anyone could get in…

"Heyo, class! Yeh know the drill… summon yer pets with the button, an' find the bush that looks like that animal!" Rewndo announced.

Ally pressed her button, and Aristar glided smoothly down from her dorm balcony. She guided him over to the hedge shaped like a black lab. Cyrus guided Ediz over to the elephant-shaped bush, but Ediz walked too far and completely knocked the hedge over.

"Um, Sir Rewndo? We don't have pets," said Emerald, stepping forward with her sisters.

"I thought you had a chameleon," Mike said coolly from over by the Irish wolfhound hedge.

"Um… yeah… er…" Sapphire stammered. "Well…"

"Eh? Princ'pal Washi'rota never fergets to give studen's pets," said Rewndo. "Why don'tcha go and' talk to him abou' it?"

And so Ally watched as the triplets ran across the dueling fields and back towards the building.

Every class was like those two. In their History of Dueling class, they didn't have any of the required books. In Dueling Sports, they had neither the proper sports gear nor their dueling pets.

But Ally's first full day back flew by, and she soon found herself back in her dorm room. She changed into pajamas, turned out the lights and went to bed.

She thought she would fall asleep immediately, but it turned out to be the opposite. Her bed was comfortable, it had been a busy day, and it was getting late, so she should've been able to fall asleep quickly. But nonetheless, she just laid in bed, staring at the clock on her nightstand, watching the hours drag on.

Why couldn't she sleep? She soon became aware of the reason; she began to hear a faint sound, much like the one she had heard on the night of Aristar's birthday. In fact, the more she listened, she started to realize that it was exactly the song that she had heard that night.

Ally tried to ignore it, but it only got louder. She smashed her pillows up against her ears, but nothing seemed to work. Extremely annoyed and frustrated, she sat bolt upright. Lydia had done the same.

"Do you hear that?" Ally asked.

"Uh-huh," Lydia replied.

Ally got out of bed, slid her feet into her dog slippers (which barked every time she took a step), grabbed a flashlight from the drawer of her nightstand and started towards the door.

"Where are you going?" Lydia asked.

"To find whoever's singing," Ally said brusquely.

"Then I'm coming, too," said Lydia confidently. Ally turned the doorknob and pulled open the heavy door to find Mike and Cyrus standing outside.

"What are you two doing here??" Lydia whisper-shouted. "Hold on… do you hear it too?"

"Yeah," said Cyrus in a hushed tone. "But it seems like we're the only ones who do… "

Ally peered down the dark hallway. They did, in fact, seem to be the only ones who heard it—or at the very least, the only ones who wanted to do something about it.

"Well, you three can stay here if you want, but I'm going to investigate," said Ally. She started walking in the direction of where the song was coming from.

Her friends had caught up with her in a matter of seconds.

"I bet it's one of those new triplets," Mike muttered as they crept down the silent (except for the sound of Ally's slippers barking), dark, deserted corridor.

"I've heard this song before," Ally whispered. "In my backyard, just a few minutes before Aristar and I left. It wouldn't make sense if it were one of the three sisters, because they were nowhere near me."

"They're nowhere near us right now and the walls are soundproof, but we can still hear whoever's singing," said Lydia quietly.

The four of them got on the elevator. Ally pressed the button that would take them to the flight range on the roof; if the song was louder on an earlier floor, they would stop there instead.

But the song seemed to be getting louder the higher they went. Soon, the elevator doors slid open with a *ding,* and Ally, Lydia, Mike and Cyrus stepped out onto the top floor of the school. It was a short hallway with a door opposite the elevator, which led out onto the roof.

Mike bolted over to the door and put his ear up next to it. He beckoned the rest of them over.

"It *has* to be coming from out there," he muttered.

Ally listened for a moment. It was definitely coming from outside on the roof.

"Which one of us is going to go out there?" asked Cyrus.

"I will," Ally said bravely.

"Just… don't die," said Lydia.

Ally opened the door and stepped out onto the roof. Her jaw dropped as soon as she did.

Sapphire was standing directly across from her with her back turned, staring up at the moon and singing the mysterious song.

Ally thought back to when she had heard this captivating song in her backyard… it had messed with her mind. She had seen all she had needed to see and didn't want the song's effects to take over her mind again. And if Sapphire caught her, she would be in big trouble.

So Ally turned around to go back into the building, but the door was already shut. She tried to open it, but it had locked itself.

This wasn't looking good. Biting her lip, Ally jiggled the doorknob frantically, but it was no use. She looked over her shoulder at Sapphire, who still seemed to be completely oblivious to Ally's presence.

*What should I do?* Ally thought, starting to panic. She took a step away from the door, and her slippers barked again. She angrily kicked those off, feeling lucky that Sapphire hadn't heard . *I could hope that our balcony is open and call Aristar… no, Sapphire would notice that for sure… I could jump off the roof… nope, I would die… I could just let Sapphire see me… no, that would end just as badly…*

And that's when she started to feel dizzy. The effects of the song were starting to kick in.

Ally couldn't think straight. Her vision went blurry, and she could barely balance. She tried to fight it, but it was just too strong.

The music flowed in through her ears and took control of her mind. She forgot where she was. What she was doing. Who she was. The song continued to hold her captive until she felt the last of her strength leave her.

Ally lost her balance and nearly fell head first onto the ground. But she felt a pair of hands grab her and drag her back into the building.

Through the lingering effects of the song, Ally heard someone calling her name. It grew louder and louder until she came to her senses and realized that it was her friends. She was back inside, and the door was shut so that the song was muffled.

"Well, something is *definitely* up with those triplets," she said.

The four of them returned to bed, all kept awake by the mystery of the triplets.

## CHAPTER FIVE

# A Willow Reins Mystery

THE NEXT DAY, ALLY'S FIRST TWO CLASSES WENT BY QUICKLY. But she was beginning to notice a strange trend: the triplets were absent from both Protection Skills and Pet Care, as well as her third class, History of Dueling.

Ally and her friends sat in class, pulling out their textbooks as the teacher, Madame Kelzen, took attendance.

"Levi?"

"Here."

"Rayna?"

"Here!"

"Ruby?"

There was no response. The teacher tried again.

"Ruby Trivala? Sapphire? Emerald?"

Still, there was no response from any of them.

"Okay, very well then, we'll just have to move on," said Madame Kelzen. "Aryanna?"

Again, there was no response. "Wow, so many people are missing today! Anyways, turn to Page 89."

Ally flipped to that page in her textbook. Just then, Lydia slid a note across the table to her. Ally read it to herself:

*Where do you think the triplets are?*

Ally took out her pencil and wrote a response.

*I don't know… maybe Sapphire saw me last night and the three of them are worried about us confronting them or something?*

Ally passed the note to Mike, who scrawled down another message and then tossed it over to Cyrus. He wrote something and then slid it back to Lydia, who did the same and passed it to Ally. She read over the notes and wrote down her own response.

*But if she had noticed you, wouldn't she have done something?*

*Yeah… they don't seem like ones that would just let that happen without doing anything about it…*

*I agree. Something doesn't add up. Hmm… may*

"*Ahem,* Miss Lancaster. Can you please answer the question?" Madame Kelzen interrupted sternly.

Ally brushed the note off of the table quickly.

"Er—well…I don't know…"

"Passing notes is against the rules. Please pay attention next time," Madame Kelzen sighed impatiently.

The rest of the day went by quickly and soon Ally was back in her dorm room, feeding Aristar his dinner.

"I just don't get it," said Lydia, who was pacing around the room, rapidly flipping through the pages of *The Willow Reins Student Handbook.* "Those triplets definitely don't seem like they belong here, but I can't figure out a way that they could have gotten past the guards. They can easily detect dark magic and stop it from getting past the gates of the school…"

"Maybe the triplets got in using really, really, really *strong* dark magic. Like Zortavka's magic," Ally suggested.

Lydia slammed the book shut and sighed heavily. "But you defeated her last year! And even if Zortavka is still alive, she's nowhere *near* strong enough to make it past the guards here."

"Maybe that's why she sent a few of her servants to do it for her," suggested Ally.

"But *why* would she want to break in?" asked Lydia.

Ally thought for a minute. But she didn't have time to respond, because suddenly, the principal's voice came on over the P.A. system.

"All students and staff, please report to the cafeteria for dinner and an emergency assembly," he said, sounding serious. "Leave your pets in your dorm rooms, it's going to be crowded."

"I bet this is about the triplets," Ally said excitedly. "Maybe we'll find out more about where they've been all day!"

"Maybe," said Lydia. The two of them left the girls' dormitories together and met Mike and Cyrus at their normal table in the cafeteria. Every seat in the cafeteria was occupied, because the whole school was there. There was so much loud talking that Ally could barely hear herself think.

"ATTENTION!" Washiarota called. "I apologize for making you all come here during your free time, but this is important. Three of our new second-year students have gone missing."

Everyone in the audience gasped.

"I knew it," Ally said under her breath.

"And as many of you know, last year, we had five of our youngest students go missing at the beginning of the year. They got themselves into very grave danger, and only returned at the end of the school year. To prevent this from happening again, we would like to send a small group of either teachers or seventh-year students on a quest to go out and find them before they get hurt. The only evidence we have of where they might have disappeared to was a note that they passed in class that reads *Gelesca Cove.* To get to Gelesca Cove you would have to sail 500 miles across the treacherous Sea of Sirens, which is home to monsters of all sorts. Without further ado… any volunteers?". Ally looked over to the seventh-years and teachers. Ari looked to be considering it, but other than that, nobody volunteered.

Without really thinking it through, Ally stood up.

"I accept the quest," she said bravely. Nobody spoke for a moment.

"Sit down, you just want to be in the spotlight again!" someone shouted.

"Yeah, you had your chance last year!" yelled another.

"Wha—? Hey! I was the one who *saved* you all last year!" Ally spat.

"Ally, *what are you thinking*??" Lydia hissed.

"I admire your bravery, Miss Lancaster, but you're just too young," said Washiarota sympathetically, making Ally feel like a fool. She stubbornly sat back down. "It appears we have no other volunteers…we'll have to figure something else out. Well, you all are dismissed. Have a good night."

*"Too young?"* Ally ranted, outraged, as she, Lydia, Mike and Cyrus left the cafeteria. "We weren't too young to save the *entire school* last year! That's it. We're going to Gelesca Cove to find those triplets!"

"Ally, you're *insane!"* said Lydia. "Do you have any idea whatsoever of how dangerous this is?"

"It'll be even more dangerous if those triplets really are evil, and are plotting something against the school now that they've picked up a lot of information on it," Ally explained.

"Makes sense to me," said Mike. "I'm in!"

"But how would we cross the ocean?" questioned Cyrus.

"It sounded like Washiarota had it all planned out," said Ally. "I bet that there are boats of some sort hidden around here…if only one of us had read *Secrets of Willow Reins…"*

Everyone looked to Lydia. She looked taken aback.

"No! I refuse to help you three out on a mission that will surely get all of us killed," she said firmly.

"You said the same thing last year," said Ally. "And yet here we are, the heroes of the school!"

Lydia sighed. *"Fine.* Inside of Principal Washiarota's office, there's a door. That door leads out to the boats."

"Then that's where we're going," Ally smirked. The four of them set off towards the principal's office.

52

## CHAPTER SIX

53

# The Ship

THE FOUR OF THEM ARRIVED AT THE MASSIVE DOORS OF PRINCIPAL WASHIAROTA'S OFFICE. "It's locked. How are we supposed to get in?" asked Mike cluelessly.

Ally thought for a minute. "Aristar, *lock pick*."

A small needle came from Aristar's collar, and Ally used it to pick the enormous lock on the doors. She pushed the doors open quietly, and everyone followed her into the office.

Ally looked around. It looked similar to how she had pictured it: an elegant desk with a bunch of papers stacked on top of it, a fancy golden chair behind it, and ornate, gold-framed pictures of dueling swords and shields along the walls. But Ally didn't see the door that would take them to the ships.

"Maybe it's hidden, so that students can't easily find it and sail away…?" Lydia suggested.

So they all started searching for a door of some sort. After looking behind every shelf, every painting and under every piece of furniture, Ally decided that there really was no door.

She leaned against the wall. "Lydia, are you sure you read that ri—?" she began, but the wall behind her suddenly started rumbling.

Ally whipped around and stepped away from the wall. Everyone froze, watching as paintings began falling from the walls. The room started quaking like crazy. And suddenly, the wall split in half.

Slowly, the two halves of the wall slid apart like elevator doors, revealing a pitch-black passageway behind it.

"Whoa," Mike murmured.

Ally peered down the dark, eerie passageway and the salty smell of seawater filled her nose. "The ships have to be down here," she muttered. She started walking down the tunnel, Aristar by her side.

As soon as Ally set foot in the creepy passageway, there was a flash of light. Torches lined the walls, and all of them had just lit themselves on fire.

Cautiously, Ally began walking down the tunnel. Her friends and their pets soon joined her. Ediz had to duck down low to fit in the passage. Once all of them were in, the walls slid shut, locking them inside the tunnel. All of the torches' flames were put out with a *whoosh* sound.

"Now what do we do?" asked Lydia quietly.

"We keep going, I guess?" replied Ally. "Wait. Aristar, torch." A lit torch came out of Aristar's collar, and Ally took hold of it. She led the group down the tunnel by the light of the torch. Before long, Ally saw a different light at the end of the tunnel. It had to be the room with the ships inside! Ally set off in a run down the rest of the passageway.

"Ally, what is—whoa," Cyrus said breathlessly when they caught up with Ally at the end of the tunnel.

The floor was flooded with water, which was a bit past ankle deep. The entire room was made of damp rock, and on one side of the huge room was a giant waterfall. This was the entrance to the Sea of Sirens.

But that wasn't the coolest part. What instantly grabbed Ally's attention was the enormous ship in the center of the room.

The ship had three tall masts, and the sails were rolled up. There was a ladder to board the boat, and wooden staircases to the two upper levels on both sides of the ship. Painted on the side of the boat in blue cursive letters were the words 'The Rovast'.

Aristar flew out from behind Ally and glided towards the boat. He landed on the crow's nest in the middle of the ship. He barked, as if telling them to board the boat.

"I guess let's go…?" said Lydia hesitantly. They all climbed aboard the ship, and so did Biggie, Ediz and Wiggles.

It was even bigger than it looked from the outside. The first thing that Ally wanted to check out was the captain's wheel. It was on one of the upper floors, so she climbed the short wooden staircase and curiously strode over to the wheel. There was a message taped to it.

The message read:

*Dear Sailors, whoever you may be,*

*I have assigned to you a mission to sail across the sea and find Ruby, Sapphire and Emerald Trivala, the second-year triplets who have mysteriously gone missing. Here are a few things to know about your journey. As tempting as it may be, never ride your pets above the ocean. The salt water can cause serious damage to their collars. If you happen to encounter a sea monster of any type, be sure to stay away from them. And finally, there is some food and gear in the bedroom.*

*Thank you kindly,*

*Principal Soren Washiarota*


Ally unfurled all of the sails by pulling a rope connected to them. The boat started to move at a slow pace out of the room… and straight towards the giant waterfall.

"Wait, we're headed straight towards the waterfall!" Mike called.

"I think that's the exit!" Ally shouted over the noise of the rushing waterfall.

And then, the waterfall split in half. Both halves of the waterfall slid apart like curtains, revealing a clear, bright blue ocean.

"It's so pretty!" exclaimed Lydia.

The boat sailed smoothly out onto the glittering water.

"Aristar, can you come here, please?" Ally called. Aristar swooped down to Ally and tilted his head. "Aristar, *map*."

A map slid out of his collar. It showed Willow Reins, and across the huge ocean it showed Gelesca Cove. It also showed a blue mark that marked where they were at.

"Great," Ally said, gazing out at the vast ocean. "Just 500 miles to go."

## CHAPTER SEVEN

# The Seven Seas

THE GROUP HAD DECIDED THAT THEY WOULD TAKE TURNS DOING JOBS ON THE BOAT: one person would captain the ship, one would keep lookout from above, another would captain the ship overnight, and the last would just walk around and make sure that everything was in order.

Today, Mike would captain during the day. Lydia would captain overnight, and Cyrus would walk around making sure everything was in order. Ally was first in line to keep lookout from the crow's nest.

They had discovered that the ship had a lower level with bedrooms on each end of the ship. Ally had insisted on staying up and sailing the ship last night while everyone else got some rest.

"See anything, Ally?" Cyrus called. Ally looked through a pair of binoculars that had come from Aristar's collar.

"Nope," Ally replied. "Just water. Water, water, and... wait, I think I see something...! Nope. Just water."

Ally, getting bored of her job, put the binoculars down and climbed down the ladder. The wind was strong, which made it harder to climb down from the crow's nest. The sails cracked and snapped in the breeze, and birds cawed noisily from above. It was a hot and humid day, and they couldn't see Willow Reins at all now. Just calm blue water in every direction.

"This might get boring after a while," said Lydia. "Just being stuck on this ship all the time..."

"Nobody said we have to stay on the ship," said Ally.

"But we're in the middle of the ocean. It's dangerous to swim," said Cyrus.

Just then, there was a very loud *SPLASH*. Ally, Lydia, and Cyrus rushed to the rail on the side of the boat and leaned over it to see what had splashed into the water.

*"Ediz!"*

Sure enough, the giant winged elephant was doggy paddling in circles in the water. Ally remembered the message that Principal Washiarota had left for them.

"Does he have his collar on?" Ally asked. Lydia squinted down at Ediz.

"Doesn't look like it," Lydia replied.

"I think his collar is up on the front of the boat," Mike yelled from the captain's seat. "I see it!"

Cyrus went to get Ediz's collar from the upper deck. When Ally turned around, Aristar was sitting right behind her with his head tilted to one side.

"You want to go swimming with Ediz, don't you?" Ally groaned. Aristar woofed, wagging his tail. So Ally removed his collar. Aristar leapt right over the railing and dove gracefuly into the water. "Be careful!" she called down to Aristar.

"Remember, when the pets don't have their collars on, they don't listen as well," Lydia reminded Ally. "Without their collars, they become…well, normal animals."

"With wings," Ally added. "That part definitely isn't normal."

Before long, the sun started to disappear behind the clouds, replaced by a full moon and a dark sky. At night, the waters became rougher.

Ally took a turn sailing for a while. For someone who was sailing for the first time ever, Ally wasn't horrible at it. For some odd reason, it all felt right—the wind smacking her face, the waves breaking over the prow.

Though after a while, the sea became so bumpy that sailing was useless. Ally got up, strode over to the railing, and watched the horizon.

"Why did the ocean get so rough all of a sudden?" Ally asked when Lydia joined her.

"Hmm… this *is* a sea full of monsters… maybe it's a Triacontapus?" Lydia suggested.

"A Tria-conta-*what now*??" Ally asked blankly.

Lydia pulled out a book titled *Sink or Swim* and flipped to page 96. "*Pronunciation: (TREE-uh-conta-pus). Noun. Meaning: an enormous, squid-like monster that destroys ships.* There, at the top of the page," Lydia read aloud. "When one senses a ship, it will come up near the surface, causing the entire ocean to go bonkers."

"That's… alarming," Ally said.

"Do we have any food?" Mike interrupted. "I'm *starving*."

Ally thought for a second. They certainly couldn't go this entire trip without food. But then she remembered part of Principal Washiarota's message:

*There is some food and gear in the bedroom.*

"I think there's some food in the bedroom," Ally said. She opened the wooden door that led to the bedroom under the captain's wheel. There were two large crates in the corner of the room that Ally looked into. One of the two contained chicken strips, mashed potatoes, fresh fruit and vegetables, granola bars, bottled water and some candy. The other probably held the gear. Ally carried the food crate outside and set it down.

"How did this stay fresh?" asked Lydia, picking up an apple that looked perfectly ripe.

"Ever-fresh crate," Cyrus read off the side of the crate. "Weird."

Ally took a container of chicken strips out of the crate. She opened it to discover that the chicken strips were steaming, as if they'd just come off the grill.

Before long, everyone was gathered around a torch from Aristar's collar, their paper plates filled with chicken strips and mashed potatoes. It was nearly impossible to eat, with how violently the ship jerked back and forth. And if that didn't make it hard enough, the ship kept plowing into massive waves, giving everyone aboard a shower. Ediz slid straight across the boat every time it jerked to the side.

"Come to think of it, has anyone seen Mokona yet this year?" Ally asked, just as the boat was thrown to the side and her food went flying out of her hands.

"I haven't seen her in any of our classes this year," said Mike.

"Neither have I," Lydia said, her tone concerned. "I don't recall even hearing her name when the teachers took attendance."

"Well, there's nothing we can do about that at the moment, so let's talk about something else," Cyrus suggested. "Do you think we'll actually make it to Gelesca Cove?"

"So far, I think we're on the right track," said Mike. "I think we can make it. Unless something insane happens, like a giant sea monster attacking us or something."

"But that'll never happen," said Ally as Ediz slid past them. Everyone agreed, though nobody truly believed it.

Lydia picked up the map and pointed to the blue dot that showed where they were. "We're about 100 miles away from Willow Reins now. We have 400 more miles to go. So if we can sail 100 miles a day, if all goes as planned, we'll be there in about 4 days."

"Not terrible," said Cyrus.

"I'm exhausted," Ally yawned. "Lydia, are you good to sail the ship overnight?"

"Wait. What?" Lydia asked. "I have to sail this thingy overnight?"

"Yes, Lydia—that's been the plan for a while now," Ally replied.

"Oh, ok," Lydia said, as though she hadn't paid any attention to the plan.

Ally entered the bedroom below the captain's wheel. Aristar followed her in. There were two small beds with striped bedding. They were both bolted to the floor so that they wouldn't slide across the room when the ship was moving. Ally got into the bed on the left, and Aristar curled up at the foot of the bed.

Ally heard a huge wave splash over the boat. She thought about that Triacontapus monster that Lydia had described.

*What if the monster senses* our *boat?* Ally thought. *What if we're under attack? We'll never make it to Gelesca Cove if it destroys our ship! What if Aristar's collar gets splashed? What if our ship goes down? What if... what if... WHAT IF...?*

Ally tried to stop thinking about those horrible ideas and think about positive things. *Our ship won't sink, it's super strong... Aristar's collar will be fine... there are probably plenty of ships in this ocean, the monster probably isn't attracted to ours... we'll be just fine...!*

She had no idea what the next day would bring.

## CHAPTER EIGHT

# The Triacontapus

THE NEXT MORNING, ALLY WOKE UP TO THE SCENT OF... *PANCAKES?* She left the bedroom to find that Aristar had what looked like a portable stove in front of him. He had a frying pan and spatula attached to his collar, and he was using a mechanical hand to flip chocolate chip pancakes over the stove. Wiggles was using gadgets from his collar to put pancakes on plates. Biggie had a tube of whipped cream in his mouth and was putting blobs of it on every pancake. There was some upbeat music playing from Ediz's collar, which he was dancing to (instead helping with the breakfast assembly line).

"It's a new feature that was added to every pet's collar!" Mike exclaimed. "It's called *meal assembly line*."

Ally accepted a pancake from Biggie, and Lydia walked over to her. She showed Ally her wristband. There was a notification on the screen that said,

*A new command has been added to every pet's collar! If you'd like to enjoy a delicious meal, but it's too complicated for your pet to cook alone, gather some of your friends' pets, and tell your pet, "[Pet's name], meal assembly line. All of the pets will work together to cook you a delicious meal!"*

"That's cool!" Ally said. "So, what will the jobs be for today?"

"I want to be the person that walks around doing nothing," declared Mike.

"I haven't captained the ship yet," said Ally. "So I'll do that."

"I can captain overnight," Cyrus said.

"And I suppose I'll be the lookout person," said Lydia.

When everyone was finished with breakfast, they all headed to their places. But first, Ally made a quick pit stop to her bedroom—she was eager to find some new gear, rather than her school uniform.

*Ooh, jackpot.* Ally grinned as she rummaged through the crate of gear.

A minute later, she strutted out wearing a black pirate's hat, a long red pirate's jacket, fingerless fighting gloves and combat boots. She also carried her trusty sword and shield.

As soon as her friends found out about this new gear, they ended up looking like a crew of pirates.

Everyone returned to their places. Ally spread the map out on the ground beside the wheel. According to the map, they had completed a bit more than one fifth of the journey to Gelesca Cove, and they were still on the right track to arrive in three or four days.

The day brought heavy winds and cloudy skies. The Rovast moved at a fast pace, due to the strong wind. But the ocean was much calmer than it had been the previous night…the whole Triacontapus thing must have just been a false alarm.

Lydia was busy keeping lookout, Cyrus was trying to teach Ediz a lesson on how to be helpful, Mike was trying (unsuccessfully) to train Biggie to do a triple backflip, and Aristar swooped in and out of the water alongside the fast-moving boat.

After a while, things became…not so calm.

"Um…I think I just saw something out in the water," Lydia reported uneasily. She climbed down from the lookout point and walked to the railing to investigate up close.

"What was it?" Mike asked, turning his head to the water.

"It looked like a…a tentacle, or something," Lydia said, sounding very worried. "Look, there it is again!"

Out on the water, Ally could see a giant tentacle-looking thing moving around. It was pretty far from their ship, though. Her mind instantly went back to the Triacontapus theory, but she didn't want to believe it. "Well, it's probably nothing," Ally said with a forced smile. "We'll just go around it. It's not harming us, so why worry about it??" She grabbed the wheel and spun it around a few times until The Rovast turned halfway to the side.

"Now it looks like there's…multiple of those tentacle things," Lydia called. "Oh, wow, there's a *lot*!"

Cyrus bolted to the railing of the ship to see the giant tentacles. Mike and Ally followed. Lydia studied the enormous tentacles carefully. But soon she gasped, cupping a hand over her mouth.

"Oh no, this is *bad*. This is very, *very* bad," she murmured.

"What? What is it?" Mike interrogated.

"It's a…a Great Triacontapus," Lydia replied nervously, her voice slightly shaky. "It's like an octopus. But approximately three hundred times bigger and with thirty huge tentacles. And according to *Sink or Swim,* the Triacontapus' only goal is to destroy all of the ships that cross the ocean."

"*All* ships?" Mike gulped.

"Is it just me, or are those tentacles getting closer to us??" Ally panicked, stepping away from the railing.

"Yup. They are *definitely* getting closer," said Cyrus, walking cautiously backward.

"Wait, I don't see them anymore…" Ally said skeptically, gripping the hilt of her sword, just to be safe.

There was a long moment of silence. Then, the ship was thrown into the air. Ally, Lydia, Mike and Cyrus all dove to the ground and wrapped their arms around the railing in order to keep from sliding off. The ship was tossed back down into the water like a toy in a bathtub, causing a huge splash that got everyone soaked.

"I think it found us!" cried Ally.

With that, a giant purple tentacle emerged from the water and slapped across the middle of the boat. Mike had to roll out of the way to dodge it.

Ally pulled her sword out and slashed the tentacle in half. She turned to her friends, who were all still on the floor. "We're under attack. Get your swords!"

Another enormous tentacle came up from the surface of the sea and knocked down the far-right mast. The wood cracked, and the mast splashed into the ocean.

More and more tentacles arose from every direction. One came speeding right at Ally. She didn't have time to dodge it; it hit her hard in the stomach, knocking the wind out of her. Ally dropped her sword as the tentacle slammed her back against a wooden wall.

The tentacle wouldn't let Ally go. Whenever she tried to break free, the tentacle just pressed her harder against the wall.

Suddenly, from above, Ally saw Lydia grab a rope. She swung down on the rope and kicked the tentacle away from Ally.

Lydia landed and pulled out her sword. She raced over to help Cyrus with a tentacle that was twice as huge as all the others.

Ally continued fighting the Triacontapus. But suddenly, to everyone's horror, there was a loud *SNAP*. A long crack ran down the center of the ship.

"We have to keep fighting!" Mike yelled. "Don't worry about tha—" But then, one of the tentacles knocked him to the ground and pinned him there. It wouldn't let him up.

Ally darted over, leaping over tentacles to get there, and then slashed the tentacle apart. As she helped Mike up, they heard another worrisome *SNAP*.

A tentacle that was WAY bigger than the rest crashed down on the middle of the boat. The boat snapped entirely in half, and both halves lifted up under the weight of the tentacle. Ally, Lydia, Mike and Cyrus all scrambled to the nose of the boat to keep away from the monster. They grabbed the tip of the ship—If they let go, they would fall into the dangerous ocean and the wreck of the Rovast.

Ally grasped the nose of the boat for dear life. The side of the boat that they were on was completely vertical, so Ally's feet dangled above the wreck.

*This is the worst thing that could've possibly happened,* Ally thought. *We'll never make it to Gelesca Cove now. We don't even have a—*

The side that the four of them were on snapped again. The nose of the boat fell into the water, taking Ally, Lydia, Mike and Cyrus with it.

When Ally splashed down into the sea, she fell with so much force that she sunk down about ten feet. She looked around for her friends, even though the saltwater stung her eyes. She couldn't see them anywhere. She tried to swim back up, but then a wooden floorboard of the Rovast floated over her and trapped her underwater. *Don't…Give…In….*Ally thought determinedly. But all the determination in the world couldn't help her. It was hopeless; Ally couldn't breathe.

She didn't know what happened next, because everything went dark.

## CHAPTER NINE

# Kalomono Sands

THE FIRST THING THAT ALLY HEARD WHEN SHE WOKE UP WAS PANTING. She sat up. It took her a second to realize where she was–she had been lying in the sand. She looked around. In front of her was the ocean, and behind her was a small forest. Aristar was next to her, panting as he dug a hole in the sand.

Ally stood up and shook all the sand off of herself. She was completely dry, so she suspected that she had washed up on this island a few hours ago or more.

She gradually began to remember everything that had happened before she lost conciousness underwater.

At first, Ally, Lydia, Mike and Cyrus went on an oversea expedition to Gelesca Cove to find Ruby, Sapphire, and Emerald Trivala, three new students that had mysteriously gone missing on the second day of school.

They boarded a ship called The Rovast. There was one successful day on the boat. But the next day, the ship was attacked by an enormous 30-tentacled sea monster called a Triacontapus.

Everyone fell into the water, and Ally passed out. And now, Ally and Aristar had somehow wound up on this island.

*Where are Lydia, Mike and Cyrus?* Ally thought. *Are they OK? And what about Wiggles, Ediz and Biggie? Are they with them?*

Ally turned to Aristar, who immediately turned his attention to Ally and away from the giant hole he had been digging.

"Aristar, where are we?" Ally asked. The island was certainly too small to be Gelesca Cove.

A note slipped out of Aristar's collar. Ally picked it up out of the sand and read it.

*Kalomono Sands.*

Ally stuffed the note into the pocket of her pirate's jacket. She started walking along the beach, looking for her friends, or any inhabitants of the island.

"Hello?" Ally called. She knew that she wouldn't receive an answer, but it was worth a try.

No response. Just as she had expected.

"Anyone here?? I'm guessing probably not, because this island is in the middle of absolutely nowhere! And it's too small to live on…but if there's another human being on this island, that would be nice…!"

She was trapped on this island, with no mode of transportation to get her off of it. Kalomono Sands was a fairly small island. Ally could see the other end of the island behind some of the trees in the small forest. She could also see a different island pretty far away. Maybe that was where her friends ended up?

She continued walking down the beach, trying to think of a plan to get off this island. She couldn't ride Aristar; it was too risky, Aristar could accidentally fly into the water. She couldn't swim to the other island; the ocean was far too dangerous. Maybe she could  build paddles and a raft of some sort and use that to get to the next island over? Or maybe she didn't have to build them–she could ask Aristar for them!

But just as she was coming up with a great plan, something hit her hard on the back of her head. She fell face-first into the sand.

"Oww!" Ally growled.

"Oops! Sorry!" said a familiar voice behind her.

Ally picked herself up and turned to face the girl that had apparently hit her with a wooden paddle. She had long, blazing red hair with emerald green tips. Her eyes were a shade of green that matched the tips of her hair, and she looked to be about Ally's age.

"Who are you?" Ally demanded, rubbing her head where she had been hit with the paddle.

"Wait, do I recognize you?" the girl yelled, stepping backward and looking stunned.

"I don't know! All I need to know is the reason you hit me with a paddle!" Ally yelled.

"Why are we yelling?" the girl shouted.

Ally cleared her throat. "Sorry. I wasn't expecting anyone else to be here. I'm Ally Lancaster. What's your name?"

"I'm Camilla Dariva," she replied. "And you don't remember how I saved your life back in the Everloushe Forest??"

"Oh, wait, now I remember you! You're the one that likes to swing on vines saving people in the forest!" Ally said. "Why exactly are you here, though? I thought the Dariva Castle was in the woods."

"Do you remember that staff that I used to teleport you and your friends back to that school?" Camilla said. "Well, Cody—my brother, in case you don't remember— and I were out in the forest looking for monsters and such, and then a Skelesnake caught us off guard. It snapped the staff in half. We had to use the staff to teleport back to the castle, so when we defeated the Skelesnake, I picked up the broken staff and said the words to teleport. But because the staff was broken, I ended up here instead."

"Wow," Ally said when Camilla finished. "Do you have the staff with you?"

"Yes, it's over there," Camilla replied, pointing at a ruby-tipped golden scepter that lay uselessly in the sand. It was completely snapped in half.

"Why are you here, though?" Camilla asked. "Isn't the school year at Willow Reins still going on?"

"It's a long story," Ally said. "So my friends—you met them—and I were sent on a mission by the principal to get to Gelesca Cove—"

"That's a horrible idea!" Camilla said in a horrified tone. "First of all, Gelesca Cove is the most dangerous island in the sea. Strange things happen there. Next, these waters are really rocky, making it very hard for a ship of any size to navigate. And lastly, this is the one week of the year that the most dangerous sea monster comes out of hiding to destroy boats—the *Triacontapus.*"

"Yeah, I know about that part," Ally said, rolling her eyes.

"You can't get to Gelesca Cove the easy way," Camilla pulled a map out of her pocket, and traced a path from Kalomono Sands to Gelesca Cove. "See, this is the more obvious way that most sailors will go. But that's where the waters get too rocky. But if you go *this* way..." Camilla traced a different, more complex path with her finger, "you'll be able to avoid the rocky part, and sail smoothly to Gelesca Cove."

"Ok, thanks," Ally said. "But I have no transportation to get there."

"Can't you ride your flying dog?" Camilla asked. "Isn't that him, flinging sand everywhere?"

"I can't get his collar wet," said Ally. "It could break it, maybe even permanently. Then I'd lose my primary source of food and transportation and…lots of other things. I know, I could just fly above the water, but I don't want to take any chances."

"Ok. If we can get my staff fixed, then I can get you a boat of some sort," said Camilla.

"Aristar, come over here, please," Ally called. Aristar trotted over to Ally and Camilla, covered from head to paw in sand. "Is there a way you can fix that scepter?" Ally pointed to the broken staff.

Aristar ran over to the scepter, kicking sand at the two girls with every step. He lowered his head and sniffed it. Then, a mechanical hand came out of his collar and lifted up the scepter. Another mechanical hand came from the other side of his collar, and it looked like it was holding some sort of golden tape. The hands wrapped the golden tape around the staff. Ally turned her head for one second, and then Aristar was in front of them with the repaired scepter in his mouth.

"Your dog is amazing," Camilla said in awe as she took the staff from Aristar. "Can't you get a boat from him?"

"Can you imagine a boat built for four people, three giant animals and one enormous elephant coming out of a collar?" Ally asked.

"You've got a point," said Camilla. "Well, what kind of boat would you like?"

"Just a small one," Ally replied. "Don't want to attract any more Triacontapuses."

"You got it," Camilla grinned. She pointed the staff at the water and yelled, "*Aquiaskia!*"

There was a blinding flash of green as a small wooden sailboat appeared, rocking back and forth in the shallow water.

"Perfect!" said Ally, racing over to check out the sailboat.

Aristar leapt onto the sailboat alongside Ally. "Well, I suppose I should get going to find my friends," said Ally. "But before you go, I have a question," said Camilla. "Have you seen Zortavka at all lately? Rumor has it that she's on the loose again."

This brought a lot of new thoughts to Ally's mind. Where was Zortavka now? Was she doing evil things to Ruby, Sapphire and Emerald on Gelesca Cove? Was she plotting revenge against Ally?

Ally decided that worrying wouldn't help anything. "Nope," she said shortly. "Bye."

"Bye," said Camilla. She handed Ally the map.

Before she left, Ally removed Aristar's collar and placed it safely in a dry compartment of the boat. A huge gust of wind sent the sailboat speeding off the shore a lot faster than Ally had been expecting—she fell backward off the boat and splashed into the shallow water. The sailboat drifted away from her, and she had to make a running leap to board the boat again. She turned around, and in Camilla's place was a fading cloud of green. The scepter had worked and she had returned home. Ally looked down at the map and read the label of the island she was headed to: *Zyleria island.*

She turned to face the sea. "Next stop, Zyleria Island. But after that, we'll be at Gelesca Cove in no time."

## CHAPTER TEN

# Port Zyleria

THE WIND WAS STRONGER THAN ALLY HAD EVER FELT, BUT THAT WAS GOOD. It would get her to Zyleria Island in a matter of minutes.

Zyleria Island was getting closer and closer by the second. Ally could feel the wind in her hair and the cold ocean mist on her face.

As soon as they reached the grassy shore of the island, the sailboat came to a very abrupt stop, causing Ally to fall forward off it. She landed in the soft grass, which was wet with dew.

When Ally looked up, she saw mountains of gray rock. There were some large flowering trees around the portion of the island that Ally could see. The rest was hidden behind the mountains.

She felt a dog licking the back of her neck. "Aristar, you—"

Ally turned around, expecting to see Aristar, instead, Biggie was behind her, wagging his tail.

Ally stood up and patted Biggie on his huge head. Then, she heard voices.

"Where's Biggie?"

"Look! Down there!"

"Who's that?"

Then, atop the mountains, Lydia, Mike and Cyrus came into sight, followed by Ediz and Wiggles.

"Down here!" Ally called, waving both her arms around frantically to get her friends' attention.

Having spotted Ally, Cyrus and Mike climbed on to Ediz, and Lydia mounted Wiggles. They glided swiftly off the mountain and approached Ally.

"Oh thank goodness, Ally!" Lydia gasped.

"Hi...first of all, why were you guys on that mountain?" Ally asked.

"At first, we all washed up on this side of the island. Then, we went over to the other side of it to see if you had ended up there, but you hadn't. We came back here, and then we found you!" Lydia explained.

"Where did that sailboat come from?" Mike questioned, pointing at Ally's gift from Camilla.

"It's a long story," Ally said. "Well, at first, I washed up on the shore of that other island over there. It's called Kalomono Sands. And you guys remember Camilla Dariva…"

Ally told them the whole story while all the pets played together in the sand.

"That's a crazy coincidence," Cyrus remarked.

"Well, we found something interesting as well, on the other side of those mountains," said Lydia, her tone tinted with concern.

"What was it?" Ally asked.

"It's sort of easier to show you than to tell you," Mike replied questionably. With that, Ally's friends led her over the mountains, and they stopped at the top.

"Down there," Cyrus pointed downward at the other side.

Ally looked down. It looked like some sort of village, but it was covered in a thick blanket of mysterious-looking fog. Ally could barely make out the roofs of some houses and other buildings.

"I say we go down there and see what all of this fog is about," Ally declared. She mounted Aristar, and they glided downward.

As soon as Ally entered the fog, she felt a strange wave of electricity surge over her. There was definitely something unnatural about this fog.

But now that she was inside, Ally could see all of the village clearly. All of the houses, lined up along winding stone pathways, were made of white brick and covered in vines. She seemed to be standing in the entrance archway, and across from her was a fancy fountain.

"Maybe we should turn back," said Lydia. "This doesn't seem safe…" She turned around and tried to walk out of the foggy town, but the fog wouldn't let her out. It was like a force field around the town. They were trapped.

"That's not good," said Ally. "We should talk to some of the townspeople and try to find out *what in the world* is going on here."

So they started strolling down one of the stone pathways. Ally began to notice that the townspeople reacted strangely whenever she and her friends walked by.

Some of them would rush into their houses, locking the doors. Others stayed outside, but Ally could hear their frantic whispers:

*"It's a crew of pirates!"*

*"They look dangerous!"*

*"Maybe they're the ones who put this fog around the village!"*

Getting tired of this, Ally strutted over to the first townsperson she saw. "Um…what's going on here?" she asked.

The townsperson leapt about a mile backward. He ran into his house without a word. But suddenly, a girl with long, dark hair streaked with blue bolted over to her. She had ocean-blue eyes and was wearing a long blue dress. Ally recognized her immediately; this was the girl who she had rescued from the Enchanted Fortress last year, Mokona Ami.

"Ally!" she gasped. "What are you doing here??"

"Better question: why are you *here*, and not at school?" Ally asked.

"Oh…that." Mokona looked concerned. "Well, you four, come with me."

Mokona led them into a deserted alleyway between two houses. "So, I ask again, what are you doing here?"

"Well, we're on our way to Gelesca Cove, but we stopped here because this fog looked weird," replied Ally. "So…what *is* it, exactly?"

"Well, the reason why I haven't been at school is because of this fog," explained Mokona. "It's like a barrier, keeping everyone inside this town from leaving the village. You can enter, but once you're inside, you can't leave. It was put here by someone right before school started, but nobody saw who did it. And that's why any suspicious-looking visitor will be arrested until they find out who actually did it."

"And since we look like pirates, *we're* suspicious visitors," Ally said with a grimace.

"Wait. So we're going to be arrested??" Mike asked blankly.

"If someone sees you, then you could be," Moko replied nervously. "That's why you have to be *extremely* careful. You can't just wander around like that!"

"But if we're trapped here, with no way out, and nobody trusts us," said Lydia, "we're definitely going to be arrested!"

"Nobody's going to jail," Ally said impatiently. "We just need to avoid the townspeople for now. And then we'll find a way to get rid of this fog, and then we can get going to Gelesca Cove!"

"Wait! I think I've heard something about this before!" Lydia exclaimed. "It's called Forbidding Fog. It acts as a magical barrier, trapping anything inside of it. The only way to clear it is by striking the barrier with a sword that's been dipped in gold."

"Where are we going to get a golden sword?" Cyrus questioned.

"There's one that's very close to us right now, actually," said Mokona. Her tone dropped to a whisper. "It's inside the most secretive place in town—the Zyleria Fountain. The fountain secretly goes about 75 feet deep, and at the bottom lies a gold-dipped sword. Nobody knows about it except for me, and I can't swim to the bottom and retrieve it, because I don't exactly know how to swim. But I *can* use my powers to put a spell on one of you that will make you be able to breathe underwater. However, the spell will only last for one minute, so you will have to be a fast swimmer. Any volunteers?"

"Not it," Lydia, Mike and Cyrus all blurted. But not Ally.

"I'll do it," she said brusquely. She strutted out of the alleyway they were in.

"Wait! You still look like a pirate. You have to be careful!" Mokona called, but Ally was already gone.

"Ediz, *rope,*" Cyrus commanded. A long rope sprouted from Ediz' collar, and Mokona took a hold of the end of it. She tossed it into the fountain, pulling it from Ediz' collar until the end of it touched the bottom of the fountain.

"There," said Mokona. "If you run out of breath, just grab the rope, and Ediz will pull you up."

"But, frankly, should we really be trusting *Ediz* with this big of a responsibility?" Cyrus asked.

"He's the strongest, so that's that," said Mokona. "Okay, now for the spell…" There was a blinding flash of blue. "Okay, Ally, as soon as you touch the water, you will be able to breathe underwater for exactly one minute."

So Ally dove into the icy cold water of the Zyleria Fountain. It was the strangest thing, being able to breathe underwater. But she had to focus on retrieving the sword.

Ally dove deeper, deeper, and deeper into the fountain as the water grew darker, darker and darker. Soon, a faint light came into view near the bottom—the golden sword.

Ally sped up and soon reached the bottom of the fountain. She gripped the hilt of the golden sword and began swimming back upward.

Ally crashed through the surface of the water and climbed out of the fountain.

"Okay…now that that's…out of the way," she panted, "how do we get rid of the fog?"

"We have to go right up to the edge of the village and strike the fog with the sword," Mokona explained. So the five of them walked to the very edge of the town, Ally carrying the golden sword.

She struck the fog with it, and all of a sudden, the dome of fog surrounding the village cleared, revealing a clear blue sky.

Ally heard the excited gasps of the townspeople nearby. An important-looking lady—Ally guessed she was the mayor—approached them.

"You four," she said. "You saved the village! Wait, you don't look familiar…are you from here?"

"No, we're not," said Ally. "We're just visiting."

"Oh, well then, I'm Mayor Zeria. And how can we ever repay you?" Mayor Zeria asked.

Ally thought for a minute. "A way off this island would be nice."

"That's easy," said Mayor Zeria. "Please, take one of our deluxe yachts. And travel safely."

"Great! Thanks!" Ally exclaimed.

"Come on, I'll lead you to the yachts!" Mokona exclaimed. She took the group to the docks and showed them the yacht that they'd be taking.

"WHOA," Mike gaped at the enormous boat. "It's *huge!*"

Mokona laughed. "Yeah, the people of Port Zyleria are pretty awesome shipbuilders."

"We should get going. The sooner we get to Gelesca Cove, the better," said Lydia. "Thanks, Moko!"

"Thank *you*," said Mokona.

Ally, Lydia, Mike, Cyrus, and the pets boarded their new ship. As the ship drifted away from the shore, Ally turned to face the docks. Mokona had vanished. *She probably teleported to school or something,* Ally thought. *Her powers can do that, right?*

The bedrooms were huge, as was the rest of the boat. There was a pool, but Ally had had enough water for one day.

Ediz captained the boat overnight. Surprisingly, he wasn't a bad captain. Ally went to bed that night for the final time before they would arrive at Gelesca Cove.

## CHAPTER ELEVEN

# Atop the Tallest Lighthouse

"THIS IS IT. THE FINAL SHOWDOWN."

"This is going to change *everything*."

"I'm winning!"

"No way! I'm five pancakes ahead of you!"

"How long is this ridiculous pancake stacking challenge going to last?" Ally groaned, as she watched Lydia and Cyrus stack pancakes from the upper deck.

Both of their stacks were at least 6 feet tall, so they both had to stand on chairs to reach the top. Wiggles and Ediz were frantically slipping pancakes out of their collars.

"Error. Pancake jam," a robotic voice from Ediz's collar said.

"Oh, come on!" Cyrus shouted as he took Ediz's collar off and began punching it angrily.

"Now look who's five pancakes ahead!" Lydia taunted.

In anger, Cyrus lost his balance and fell backward into his pancake stack, sending all of the pancakes flying to the ground.

"This is the championship round. It could go on all day!" Mike announced into a fake microphone as if he were the commentary for this battle.

"We arrived at Gelesca Cove three hours ago. It *may* be time to stop stacking pancakes and go rescue Ruby, Sapphire and Emerald," Ally said sarcastically.

"Ohhhh, it looks like Whysperia's stack is wobbling," Mike said into the mic, ignoring everything Ally had just said and leaning on the railing of the upper deck.

"Come on," Ally said, grabbing Mike's arm and dragging him down to the lower deck where the pancake challenge was taking place. "We have to get to the triplets."

"Well, Ally's right. Better go and just declare me the winner," Cyrus said quickly, jumping off of his chair and strutting over to Ally and Mike.

"Hey, that's not—" Lydia started, but in anger, she threw her arm straight into her pancake stack and it toppled right over Ally's head.

The four of them left the yacht and stepped onto the sand of Gelesca Cove. It had some rocky cliffs near the center of the island, and the sand had a pinkish tint to it. But the thing that stood out most to Ally was the lighthouse that towered high above them. Ally guessed that it was somewhere between 300 and 400 feet tall.

"Whoa," Ally gaped at the massive structure.

"Who even *built* that thing?" Lydia pondered. "It's *incredible*."

"Incredibly *tall*," Ally added.

"Uh… guys…?" Mike said uneasily. Ally turned to face him, and he was pointing off into the distance. The yacht was slowly drifting away from the shore, and it was already a good distance away.

"No big deal. We could just ask the pets for a new boat," Cyrus shrugged.

"Not any more, we can't," Ally said. She pointed to the water. Out by the yacht, which was very far away now, were the pets, trying to get the boat back. The problem was, though, they were all diving into the water and then flying straight up out of it. This was definitely damaging their collars.

"Aristar, come back here!" Ally called.

"Wiggles! You're breaking your collar!" Lydia yelled.

"Ediz, you doofus elephant!" Cyrus shouted.

"C'mon, Biggie!" Mike hollered.

They obeyed and glided back. But sparks were shooting wildly from their collars, and Ally knew that the collars were badly broken.

"Nobody panic," Lydia said in a panicked tone. "I've been reading about Willow Reins history, and I found out how the collars work. I also found a way to fix them when they've been damaged by water. You guys can go look for the triplets and I'll work on the collars."

"Ok, that'd be a big help," Ally said with a grin.

Ally, Mike and Cyrus split up to search the island for the triplets. They searched the island all day, but there was no sign of the sisters.

By 9:00 at night, Lydia had repaired all the pets' collars. The sky was already really dark, and it was starting to rain.

The four of them and the pets were gathered in a circle in the sand. The pets' collars were fixed so that they could understand simple commands, but they were in no condition to create something as large as a yacht.

Lydia had the map spread out in front of her face, and her expression looked concerned. "The principal said that they were here. I just don't understand where they could *be...*"

"What if they're in some sort of underground bunker or something?" Mike suggested.

"Don't mean to change the subject or anything, but what's the forecast for tonight?" Cyrus asked, concerned.

"Aristar, what's the forecast for tonight?" Ally repeated to Aristar. A piece of parchment printed from his collar. It said:

9:00 PM —Storms

10:00 PM — Severe Storms

11:00 PM — Extra Severe Storms

12:00 AM— 8:00 AM — Extra Severe Storms

"We don't have any shelter," said Lydia. "We'll need to find shelter somewhere on this island."

"I know," said Mike, a bit of hesitation in his tone. "We could take shelter in that lighthouse?"

"I guess we don't really have a choice," Cyrus yelled over the intensifying storm. "We should go."

They all stood up and started towards the incredible, unnaturally-tall lighthouse.

When Ally, Lydia, Mike, Cyrus and the pets made it to the lighthouse, they discovered that the wooden door was locked.

"You can all stand back," Mike said smugly. "I'm, ah, kind of an expert with locked wooden doors. You know, after I heroically shot down the door to the Enchanted Fortress."

Mike pulled a rusty old gun from his duffel bag and pointed it at the door.

"You kept that?" Ally asked, raising an eyebrow.

Mike shushed her. Ally, Lydia and Cyrus covered their ears and within seconds, the door was in a wreck in the sand. They all stepped inside.

Once inside, Ally looked above them, and it made her head spin. Four hundred feet of spiral stairs, winding around the sides of the lighthouse. At the very top was a bright light.

"Well, this'll do," said Ally. She sat down on the cement ground and listened to the rain pelting on the walls. Ally laid down with her hands behind her head, and then realized something strange—the door was back, and in perfect condition, as if nothing had ever happened. After a few minutes, the floor began to feel strangely…wet.

Ally sat up. There was a puddle of sparkling blue-green water on the ground. It seemed to be rising, maybe one inch every 10 seconds.

"Something tells me we may want to get out of here," Ally said. "Mike, could you shoot the door down again?"

Mike picked up the old gun again, a worried expression on his face. "It's out of bullets."

The water was rising fast. Lydia waded over to the door, and tugged at the lock. Her jaw dropped, and her eyes widened in fear. "It's locked! We're trapped! What do we do, what do we do, what do we—!?"

"Look out!" Ally yelled. Lydia gasped and looked upward, frozen with fear. Ally shoved her out of the way, and the two of them hit the water just as one of the heavy concrete stairs fell right where Lydia had been standing. Then another one fell right between Mike and Cyrus, causing water and tiny concrete bits to splash over them.

Ally and Lydia came above the surface, both drenched in the sparkling water.

"We have no choice but to take the stairs," said Cyrus.

"But—" Lydia started, but Ally grabbed her hand and pulled her up the stairs. Mike and Cyrus followed.

Stairs were collapsing all around them. The water was now rising at about 5 inches per second, and it seemed almost like it was following them up. About a hundred feet up, there was a gap between two stairs. It looked as if about four stairs had fallen. Ally leapt across, grasped the next stair with her wet fingers, and pulled herself up. Then about 150 feet up, the step that Ally stepped on crumpled and fell. She dropped with the step, and just managed to grab ahold of the next step before taking a plunge into the deep, shimmering water.

"Go, go, go!" Mike shouted frantically. The water was rising so quickly now that it kept splashing against Ally's feet.

Ally looked back behind her to make sure her friends were still following, but then slipped. She hit her right cheek hard on one of the steps ahead of her, scraping it badly. The water kept rising, and it splashed against her face. She scrambled to her feet after wiping the blood off of her face and then dashed up the remaining stairs.

After lots of jumping over missing stairs they reached the top, where there was a balcony that looped around the light. It didn't have a railing, though. Exhausted and out of breath, Ally and her friends sat down on the balcony. It was still raining, but only a drizzle.

"Well, now what do we do?" Mike asked. "We could jump the 400 feet or we could drown in the weird shiny water."

"This plan was not very well thought out," Ally realized. But then, she heard something. It was a soft song, exactly like the one that she heard in her backyard and on the roof the other night.

Everything else went silent as a glowing blue shoe stepped out from behind the light. Ally looked up to find that it wasn't just a shoe—it was Sapphire.

Sapphire's normally black hair was now blue and glowing, and so was her billowing aqua-colored dress. She also wore a pale blue translucent cape, but the brightest part of her attire was the iridescent sapphire pendant on her necklace. She looked completely different from the Sapphire she had met at Willow Reins. And Ally thought she resembled someone else she knew…but she couldn't put her finger on *who*.

"What are YOU doing here?" Ally blurted stupidly, scrambling to her feet. "I thought you were just a normal student!"

"One may seem like a gem on the outside," Sapphire said calmly, smirking, "but that doesn't change anything on the inside. And I'm surprised you haven't pieced it together yet, Lancaster. The song…the sea…I thought you would've figured it out after you heard me on the roof."

"Wait, you knew I was there?" Ally asked.

"Of course I did," said Sapphire. "Your barking slippers gave you away immediately. So have you figured out our little secret yet?"

"I…uh…" Ally tried to think. What could they be hiding? The song…the sea—

"They're sirens," Lydia murmured quietly, her face going blank.

"*Gemstone* sirens," Sapphire corrected slyly.

"Just—what do you want from us, Sapphire?" Ally barked. It dawned on her that Sapphire and her sisters weren't on the good side. They were just in *disguise* as students at Willow Reins.

"To kill you," Sapphire answered shortly. Then, she unexpectedly pulled a glowing blue sword out of nowhere, did some crazy sword-spinning trick, threw the sword in the air and caught it by the hilt.

"What was your plan?" Ally asked, suddenly a bit terrified of Sapphire—or whoever she really was.

"Well, we were sent by Zortavka to get revenge on you four." Sapphire inched closer to Ally, who backed up as far as possible. "We lured you to the top of this lighthouse so that you'd have nowhere to escape."

Out the corner of her eye, Ally saw Ediz floating by. She whispered to Lydia, "You guys jump onto Ediz. I'll handle her."

Lydia gave Ally a horrified glance but then realized that Ally wasn't going to let her stay up there. So Lydia whispered the plan to the boys, and they both looked unsure about it. But when Sapphire swung the sword one more time and her eyes started glowing, the three of them immediately leapt off the balcony and landed on Ediz, who took them safely down to the ground.

Ally's eyes locked on Sapphire's blue, glowing ones. After a long moment of silence, Ally lunged at Sapphire. Sapphire fell to the balcony floor, and Ally held her to the ground. But somehow, Sapphire managed to punch Ally in the face—right where she had hit it on the hard stairs—

causing Ally to loosen her grip and giving Sapphire the chance to escape and get to her feet.

Suddenly, Sapphire started singing the same song that she had been singing on the roof. It made the world spin, and Ally had to hold on to one of the supports of the lighthouse roof to keep from falling over. She couldn't break free of the trance that the song had put her in. It only got louder…and louder…and louder…

Sapphire got closer to Ally. Ally couldn't think straight at all. Her memory was all foggy, and she forgot how she had gotten there. Then Sapphire kicked Ally right in the knee, and she stumbled backward. Until she realized that there was no ground beneath her foot.

She fell backwards off the balcony but managed to grasp the edge of the balcony with just her fingertips. She tried as hard as possible to fight the song that was holding her captive, and the world started to spin a little less. She could think almost normally again, but she definitely wasn't safe yet. Sapphire stood right on the edge of the balcony, and it looked as if she was about to step on Ally's hand. Then the shining water from inside the lighthouse started pooling on the balcony. It made it twice as hard to hold on.

Sapphire had an evil grin on her face. "Well, Lancaster, your journey has ended," she said. "Any last words?"

"Yes. If I go down—" Ally said. Using all the strength she had left, she reached up and grabbed Sapphire's ankle. "—you go down with me."

Sapphire's jaw dropped. She attempted to shake Ally off of her, but it was no use. Ally wouldn't let herself let go no matter what. She yanked hard on Sapphire's leg, and then Sapphire fell right over the edge.

Over her shoulder, Ally saw Sapphire splash into the deep sea. She was gone, and not coming back. But it was no time to be cheerful—Ally was still dangling about 400 fcct in thc air.

She just couldn't pull herself up. It was no use, anyway. The water was filling the lighthouse to the very top. It was too high up to call for one of the pets, they wouldn't be able to hear her. There was no possible escape from this situation.

Ally let go and plummeted downward just as the lighthouse exploded.

# CHAPTER TWELVE

# Trouble at the Tip of the Cove

THE DIFFERENT FEATURES OF GELESCA COVE TUMBLED IN AND OUT OF ALLY'S VISION. The wind smacked her face, harder and harder the farther she fell. She could have tried to think of a plan to save herself, but she didn't. Her mind went blank and her only thought was *"AAAAAAH!"*

Suddenly, she landed on something. But it didn't feel far enough down to be the ground, and it felt like everything was still moving.

It took Ally a moment to come to her senses and realize what had happened—Aristar had caught her. Still dazed and confused from the effects of the siren song, she gripped the fur on Aristar's neck as he brought her down safely to the beach.

When Aristar landed, Ally dismounted clumsily, stumbling forward and nearly falling flat on her face before a pair of hands grabbed her by the shoulders. Lydia turned Ally around to face her and immediately started bombarding her with questions.

"Are you hurt?" Lydia asked, sounding very concerned. "Can you hear me? Do you need bandages?"

"I'm fine," Ally said. "Even better now that we know the Sirens' secret."

"Yes," Lydia said. "But we won't be able to get much further unless we have information about where Ruby and Emerald are."

*Darn,* Ally thought, feeling a bit foolish. *I didn't even think to ask where Sapphire's sisters were.*

"All I really care about right now is that I'm alive," Ally said. "I'd most likely be dead by now if Aristar hadn't caught me."

"You're right," Lydia realized. "Follow me, we have some bandages for your face."

Ally and Aristar followed Lydia along the beach. The sky was pitch black, and the night air was cold and chilly. The only sound was the wind whistling past Ally's ears.

They made it to Mike and Cyrus, who were both staring at video games in their hands. The boys, along with their pets, were surrounding a crackling campfire. The two of them abandoned their video games and scrambled to their feet, kicking sand back all over the pets.

"We thought for sure you were dead!" Mike blurted.

"I'm not, but Sapphire's definitely not coming back," said Ally.

"Yeah, we saw her hit the water," Cyrus said. "When she went under, I'm not sure if you saw this, but a blue light appeared in that spot. It flew out of the water and towards the horizon."

"How late is it?" asked Ally, who had completely lost track of time.

"It's almost midnight," Lydia replied, checking her wristband clock. "Oh, tomorrow's Halloween. Principal Washiarota just announced it."

"Great. We're missing holidays, just like last year," said Cyrus unenthusiastically.

"We should probably get to bed, I'm absolutely exhausted," Ally yawned. Her friends agreed, and four rolled-up sleeping bags rolled off of Ediz' head. Ally picked up a blue and black one and unrolled it in the sand. Her friends chose the other ones.

"Aristar, *beach towel*," said Ally, while her friends unrolled their sleeping bags. A blue and orange paisley-patterned beach towel slid out from Aristar's collar. Ally laid it out on the ground for Aristar and he plopped down on it.

Mike and Cyrus were asleep as soon as their heads hit the ground. Lydia stayed up reading *Good as Gold* with a bright reading light from Wiggles' collar. Ally thought that because of all the crazy events tonight, that she would fall asleep almost instantly. But instead she lay awake, thinking about Sapphire and how she had pulled her into the deep sea. *What if Zortavka was just controlling an innocent person, and making them try to—*

But she didn't get the chance to finish that thought, because there was a loud *SNAP* noise.

She sat up and looked around at her friends, who were also awake.

"What was that?" Cyrus said in alarm.

"I don't know. Or care," Mike groaned carelessly. "I don't know about you guys, but I'm going back to bed."

"Well I'm not," said Lydia, promptly slamming her book shut. "Don't you remember that at night, monsters come out? We can't just go to sleep, we need to find out what that noise was."

"She's right," said Ally. Cyrus agreed. They turned to Mike, but he was already snoring. Or, more likely, fake-snoring.

Ally, Lydia and Cyrus stood up and got flashlights from their pets. They entered the woods, Aristar trailing behind them.

They clicked on the flashlights and began the search for monsters. Ally really wasn't looking for monsters, though. She was looking for the Sirens.

They crept cautiously around the woods, on high alert. The three of them had their swords in their scabbards; Ally could see that Cyrus's free hand gripped the hilt of his sword. Ally did the same, just in case any monsters jumped out of the shadows.

The ground seemed to be slightly sloped, as if they were walking up a hill. Ally wouldn't let her guard down. Lydia flinched at sudden sounds, and jumped whenever the wind blew by. Aristar trotted alongside them.

Soon, they reached a clearing. It was a large, flat patch of grass that was, in fact, on top of a hill. Ally looked down to see that they had walked up a 50-foot tall hill without really noticing.

The view from there was amazing. The full moon's reflection on the calm ocean. Shimmering water still pouring from the wrecked lighthouse like a waterfall. Mike, Wiggles, Ediz and Biggie snoring at the campsite.

Ally admired the mesmerizing view for a minute or two. Then Lydia appeared at her shoulder.

"It's beautiful," Lydia said in awe. "But did we really just climb a hill without knowing it?"

"I guess so. Kinda weird," Ally said. They seemed to be at the highest point of the island. Ally and Lydia gazed out at the ocean a little while longer.

The only sound was the crickets chirping from the woods below.

Until there was a soft growling noise.

Ally cautiously turned around to see a small, gray, wolf-like creature, poised to attack with its teeth bared. But it wasn't a normal wolf; its eyes were sparkling electric blue, while sparks of lightning flew everywhere in the space around it. Cyrus stood behind it, sword in hand, prepared to fight.

"Aristar, what is that thing?" Ally muttered to Aristar, careful not to make any sudden moves.

A note slipped out of Aristar's collar. It read: ***Electrowolf! Don't touch it!***

More electrowolves started emerging from the woods and approaching the first one from behind. Ally and Lydia drew their swords, but couldn't figure out which wolf to target, because there was a whole pack of wolves now. Suddenly, a loud stomping noise interrupted the silence. Everyone froze to listen, and the stomping was followed by a loud trumpeting sound. It was undoubtedly…an elephant.

Ediz crashed through the trees. Mike was on the elephant's back, steering Ediz to trample the electrowolves.

The electrowolves began attacking, but they were no match for Ediz's strength and size. And with Ally, Lydia,

Mike and Cyrus joining in with the battle, the wolves had no chance.

Things were going well, until out of the blue, an electrowolf lunged straight at Ally. It sent her falling backwards, towards the hill they had climbed up earlier. Ally rolled down the hill, wrestling the wolf at the same time, the wolf's claws opening gashes on her face and arms. Eventually they rolled onto the flat ground at the foot of the hill. The wolf stood over her, surely thinking it had won. But Ally had just enough strength left in her to shove the wolf out of the way and make a mad dash back up the hill.

When she returned to the top of the hill, all of the wolves seemed to have vanished.

"Where did all the…?" Ally asked.

"Ediz drove them all off," Cyrus replied.

Aristar stepped over to Ally, and a roll of bandages came out of his collar.

"Thanks," Ally said. She wrapped a bandage around her badly scratched arm.

"Ally…you have to see this," Lydia murmured. She was at the edge of the hill, staring at something in the ocean.

Ally, Mike and Cyrus skeptically came over to Lydia and followed her gaze.

In the exact spot that the lighthouse had been a few minutes ago stood a towering cliff. On top of the enormous gray rock cliff was a little red-roofed shack. Red, blue and green fog surrounded the whole thing.

Ally yelled, "That's where the sirens are hiding!"

## CHAPTER THIRTEEN

# Through the Ruby Corridor

ALLY WAS SO EAGER TO FIND THE GEMSTONE SIRENS THAT AS SOON AS SHE REALIZED THE SHACK WAS THEIR HIDING PLACE, SHE BOLTED DOWN THE HILL. Ally was out of breath by the time she reached the sand. Her hands lowered to her knees as she caught her breath.

Soon enough, her friends and all the pets came crashing through the woods behind her.

"The sirens…definitely hiding up there," Ally panted, pointing up at the shack.

"You're right," Lydia said in realization. "The red fog represents Ruby, blue is Sapphire, and green is Emerald."

"But Sapphire…I thought you tossed her into the ocean," Cyrus said.

"That doesn't mean…her sisters aren't up there," Ally gasped. She stood up straight. "We have to get up there. Let's go."

And so the four of them jogged across the sand toward the strange cliff. It seemed even taller and more intimidating every step they took. Luckily, they had the pets and wouldn't have to climb it—that was a relief.

Aristar readied his wings and let Ally mount. They took off toward the top of the cliff, closely followed by everyone else.

Aristar landed gracefully in front of the red-roofed shack, and so did Wiggles, Biggie and Ediz. Ally and her friends all dismounted.

"Is it safe? Should we go in?" Lydia questioned.

"Is it safe? Um…I'm guessing not," said Ally. "But we're going in anyway."

Ally examined the door. She put one hand on the rusted brass handle and used the other to draw her sword. Ally cautiously pulled the door open, and they all stepped tentatively inside.

It looked like a normal living room on the inside—two leather sofas, a furry rug, and paintings on the walls.

"Well, this is underwhelming," Ally said, raising an eyebrow and lowering her sword.

"Something about this just seems kinda fishy, though," Cyrus stated, narrowing his eyes and gazing around the room for traps.

"We should—" Ally began, but didn't get the chance to finish her sentence. Suddenly, a long crack spread along the center of the floor.

"Uh…something tells me we should get out of here," Lydia gulped in fear, backing away from the long crack.

"Yes, we *definitely* need to get out of here," Ally said immediately. She spun around and tried to open the door—but it was locked.

The shack began to rumble violently, and the shelves and pictures lining the walls fell, dismantled by all of the chaos.

"Here, let me try," Mike said, stepping up to the door. He first tried normally pulling it open, but that didn't seem to work. Next he rattled the handle, but that didn't do anything. Finally Mike attempted to chuck his sword at the door, but, as expected, that didn't do anything at all.

"We're locked in here," Mike said, stating the obvious.

The ground completely split into two halves. Everyone watched in shock as one of the halves crumpled and dropped entirely, unveiling a deep pit of darkness.

And then the same thing happened to the other half.

Ally, Lydia, Mike and Cyrus plummeted downward in total darkness, with no idea where they were or when this fall would end.

It was impossible to tell whether she was right-side-up or upside-down, because there was nothing but pitch-black darkness in every single direction.

*Did the Sirens lure us into a magical trap?* Ally thought in terror. *Will we just keep falling for eternity? When we land... IF we land... what will we land on? Concrete? Spikes? A pit of monsters?* Anything was possible with the Sirens, and the thought made Ally shudder.

But her theories were proven wrong when she landed on something cushion-like. This was definitely not what she had expected, and whatever this was supposed to be,

Ally detected something suspicious. The Sirens wouldn't drop them 300 feet just to land on some weird cushion.

Suddenly, the lights came on with a *boom*. Ally shielded her eyes from the bright light with her gloved hand and looked around at her new surroundings.

She, her friends, and the pets were all on a gigantic blue cushion inside a cylinder-shaped room. Beside the cushion was a doorway to another room.

*That must be where we have to go, Ally thought. Besides—the only other way is up, and that would just be going backwards. We have to get moving, there's no time to waste. I'm actually wasting time just sitting here and thinking about wasting time! I do that a lot, and really have to stop doing it. Aack—wasting even more time!*

Ally climbed across the huge cushion toward the doorway. When she reached the edge, she hopped off and walked into the next room.

"Whoa." Ally's mouth fell open as she looked around this room. It was the same tall cylinder shape as the other room, and the circular ground appeared to be made of gold. Directly across from the entrance were three long hallways. The one on the far left had a giant ruby embedded in the wall above it, and the one on the right had an emerald. The one in the center had an unidentifiable jet-black gem. Ally guessed that it was meant to take the place of the sapphire, because Sapphire had been defeated.

Ally tried to figure out what could lie at the end of these three dark passageways. *Maybe Ruby is at the end of the one with the ruby, and Emerald at the end of the emerald one, and we have to fight each of them…but that doesn't explain anything about the one in the center…maybe the gem turns black once that siren is defeated…probably not…maybe…*

"Are we really going down those dark passageways?" Lydia asked suddenly, sounding hesitant.

"Of course we are. It's the only way to complete the quest," Ally replied firmly. "Ruby and Emerald have to be hiding somewhere down here…I can tell…"

She strode over to the center of the room, and glanced back and forth between the three corridors, coming up with a plan. "Ok. So, the black gem in the middle could indicate something really dangerous, so we'll save that one for last. To me, Ruby seemed like the leader of the Sirens, and she might put up a better fight than Emerald… and that leaves…" Ally paused, thinking. "We're going down the Emerald corridor first," she decided. She began walking towards the Emerald hallway, expecting everyone else to follow.

"Sounds good to me," said Mike.

"Ugh, fine," said Lydia, sounding suddenly angry.

Ally stopped in her tracks and turned to face Lydia. "What?" she asked, raising an eyebrow.

"I'm just getting tired of you making the decisions *every single time*!" Lydia hissed.

"What do you mean by that?" Ally asked irritably.

"You just never let anyone else have the chance to be the leader," Lydia barked. "It's like you elected yourself the leader of this team, and none of us had a say in it. You're just—so—selfish sometimes!"

"Well, maybe I just make all of the decisions because I know better than you do!" Ally argued. "Besides…*someone* has to take charge, and I'm the best option." She realized that she did sound very selfish saying that.

"Can you think of one time that you let someone else be in charge? You're the one who decided to even go on this crazy mission in the first place; if you hadn't, we wouldn't have been attacked by that crazy Triacontapus thingy, and we wouldn't have almost drowned in a giant lighthouse!" Lydia ranted, pacing back and forth with hand gestures to match her words. "And last year, if you hadn't decided to run off and try to defeat the worst villain in the history of villains, Mike, Cyrus and I wouldn't have nearly died trying to do so!"

"Well, if *you* had been in charge, where would we be now?" Ally retorted. "At school, sitting around reading books or something?"

After shooting Ally one last angry look, Lydia strutted away from the group, toward the Ruby corridor.

"What are you doing?" Ally barked.

"I'm going down the Ruby hallway myself," Lydia replied furiously. "You're welcome to join me if you'd like. If not, then it just proves me right about how selfish you are."

Wiggles trailing behind her, Lydia disappeared into the dark Ruby corridor.

"Ok, let's move on to the Emerald corridor," said Mike cluelessly.

"You two can go that way if you want, but I'm going after her," said Ally. As mad as she was, she knew she couldn't just leave Lydia alone to face whatever danger was at the end of the Ruby hallway. There was a chance she could get herself killed.

Ally set off by herself down the Ruby passageway.

125

## CHAPTER FOURTEEN

# The Ruby Labyrinth

THE RUBY HALLWAY WAS MUCH LONGER THAN ALLY HAD EXPECTED. At least it gave her time to prepare herself for whatever was at the end of it.

She assumed that Mike and Cyrus would follow eventually, but whether they did or didn't, Ally had to find Lydia before she had the time to get herself into trouble. And, if possible, find Ruby.

Soon, a small light appeared in front of her—the end of the hallway. Ally sighed in relief and broke into a run down the rest of the hallway.

She came to a halt and looked around just before going into the next room. Standing before her was what appeared to be the entrance to a foggy maze with walls that stretched from floor to ceiling. But in front of the entrance was a wooden signpost with words written in blood:

*At this point you will begin a perilously puzzling challenge. Enter if you dare.*

*Warning: Danger lies ahead.*

*Just great, a maze,* Ally thought. But she began to realize something else. *Blood-written signs...where have I seen those before? Not this year...was it last year, in the...?*

She realized—that was it. Inside the Enchanted Fortress, there were signs written in blood. What worried Ally was that the signs in the Fortress had been written by none other than Zortavka, who was *the worst* villain there was.

Ally abandoned her old fears as new worries filled her mind. *Is Zortavka actually behind all of this? Could she really be using the Sirens, and luring us to her through them? What if Zortavka is hiding somewhere in the maze? Oh no…what if Lydia finds Zortavka or Ruby and has to fight them alone? What if…?*

Ally had to take action. She entered the foggy maze.

She turned a corner. But as soon as she did, a Skelesnake came out of nowhere and lunged at her face.

Caught by surprise, Ally fell to the ground. She wrestled the Skelesnake, tossed it away from her, got to her feet, and stabbed it to death with her sword.

As Ally explored the maze for hours on end, it didn't really feel like she was progressing at all. There were seemingly no dead ends, which made it feel like she was going in circles. There was also still no sign of Lydia or any of her friends.

"Lydia?" Ally called, her hands cupped around her mouth. Maybe the thick walls of the maze were soundproof, because there was no response.

"Mike?" she tried again.

No response.

"Cyrus?"

No response.

"Anyone?"

Again, no response.

Ally sighed. Was this just a never ending maze? Would she be trapped searching for a way out forever? It couldn't be—Ally wouldn't let it be.

She had to be nearing the end by now. She just had to keep moving.

Ally turned, leaping back in surprise as she rounded the corner and came to a huge wall made of fire.

She backed away and turned around, but another wall of fire was blocking that direction as well. Ally was trapped. She didn't know what to do, when suddenly, there was a bark from behind her.

"Aristar!" Ally cried, relieved at the sight of her dog. "How did you get through the...? Nevermind. Not important. We need to find a way to clear these fire walls so that we can move on."

Ally glanced back and forth between Aristar and the fiery walls, and she came up with an idea. "Aristar, *hose*."

A long hose grew from Aristar's collar, and Ally took it by the spout. Water began spraying from it, and Ally put out the wall of fire in front of her like it was nothing.

"Perfect," Ally grinned. "Now we can—Aristar?" Ally glanced over her shoulder, expecting to see Aristar trotting along behind her. To her surprise, Aristar had vanished into thin air.

"Aristar?" Ally called out, beginning to feel alarmed. There was no trace of him.

Ally had to get out of there. So she set off at a run through the rest of the maze.

After several monster battles and what felt like hours of running, Ally came to an empty, circular-shaped clearing in the maze.

There wasn't anything there. So Ally turned around to move on.

"Hello again, Ally," came a drawling voice from behind her. Ally whipped back around.

"Ruby," Ally said under her breath. Sure enough, Ruby stood in the center of the room, an evil grin on her face. Ruby looked, just as Sapphire had, entirely different from when they had first met back at Willow Reins. Her long hair had transformed from plain brown to glowing, blazing red. Her storm-gray eyes were now also red and glinting with malice. The same went for her sparkling dress, long cape, and the pendant on her necklace, which shone brighter than any other part of her outfit.

"I know what you're hiding," barked Ally instantly, drawing her sword. "You and your sisters are the Gemstone Sirens, and you work for Zortavka."

"Good. That will make this so much easier, then," Ruby smirked. She pulled a shimmering metal sword out of nowhere, held it to the sky, and it suddenly caught fire.

*Uh-oh,* thought Ally. *This isn't good.*

"Now, unlike my foolish sister…" Ruby began pacing back and forth in circles around Ally, her eyes locked on hers the whole time. "I'll give you a chance to save yourself."

"What do you mean?" Ally asked skeptically.

"If you join us—join the Dark Mistress," said Ruby. "My sisters and I—none of us will hurt you. You have a second chance. We could all be on the same side. But if you choose otherwise…" Ruby ran her finger along the edge of her sword menacingly, apparently immune to fire.

"Hmm…tough one," Ally lied, slowly stepping up closer to Ruby, lowering her sword further. "You know what?" Her eyes locked on Ruby's. "I will *never* join you."

"Very well then."

Ruby thrust her flaming sword at Ally, who narrowly dodged it by ducking backward. Ally dropped to the ground, rolled out of the way, jumped up and swung her sword at Ruby.

Ruby backflipped to dodge it and landed gracefully on her feet. Out of nowhere, she put down her sword and clutched the ruby pendant of her necklace.

"What are you…?" Ally asked suspiciously. Ruby's eyes flashed an even brighter red, and she began singing the same song Ally had heard Sapphire sing countless times before. *No, not this again,* Ally thought.

Her vision blurred, her memory went foggy and she couldn't think straight.

Ally forgot where she was. She forgot what she was doing—the whole mission, the Gemstone Sirens, everything. And…what was her name again?

Ruby's song seemed to be stronger than Sapphire's, because Ally was completely unable to fight it. It took control of her, and she could barely keep her balance. Ally heard her sword clatter to the ground—she must have dropped it. She fell to the ground.

"Looks like this is the end of the remarkable Ally Lancaster," Ruby said softly. At least, that's what it seemed like she said, because her words were all jumbled up in Ally's head.

Ruby lunged at her and pinned her to the ground.

"You know what I think?" Ruby asked. "I think you're about to die."

"Nope, probably not," Ally managed. Despite what she was saying, It occurred to her that this may just be her final resting place—a gloomy maze, defeated by Zortavka's Gemstone Sirens. She desperately wanted to break free of this mental hold that the siren song had her in and escape, but at the same time, she was too confused to do so. Ally was just about to give up all hope when—

"Hey, Ruby! Over here!" demanded a voice from the entrance of the room. Ally couldn't quite make out who the voice belonged to, but she managed to turn her head just enough to see who it was.

Ally's mouth fell open in shock. Lydia stood in the doorway, sword drawn, a confident look on her face.

"What!?" Ruby looked up from Ally.

Ally saw her chance. She rolled out of Ruby's way, grabbed her sword, leapt to her feet, and stood by Lydia's side.

"So there are two of you foolish girls, I see," Ruby said, smirking and standing up. "Good. This will make it twice as fun."

Ruby pulled out a new huge, fiery sword, tossed her head back, and cackled maniacally.

"Ally, we need a plan, and we need one *now*," Lydia muttered. "And it can't just be our usual try-to-think-of-a-plan-but-end-up-wasting-a-bunch-of-time-thinking-and-never-come-up-with-an-actual-plan kind of thing!"

"I know," Aly muttered back, nervously staring at Ruby. "But what are we even supposed to do? She's a *way* stronger enemy than Sapphire!"

"I don't know!"

"Okay, we'll just have to come up with a plan eventually," Ally whispered quickly. "Just try not to die, ok?"

Lydia looked mortified. "You think we might die?"

"Oh, nevermind! Just fight!" Ally growled. Suddenly, Ruby lunged at them. Right on time, Ally caught Ruby's weapon with her own, and the two struck against each other with a deafening *clang*.

At the same time, Ally kicked Ruby hard in the knee. She dropped her sword and staggered backward. Ally snatched Ruby's flaming sword off the ground.

"You. Give. That. Back!" Ruby demanded.

"Actually, I think I'll hold on to it," Ally grinned.

"What are you *doing*??" Lydia frantically whisper-shouted. "You're just going to make her even more angry, and—"

"Just go with it!" Ally hissed.

As predicted, Ruby charged at Ally.

"Lydia! Catch!" Ally yelled. She tossed the sword to Lydia, who caught it by the hilt.

Ally dove out of the way. She hit the ground hard, but it was much better than getting pummeled by Ruby, who slammed head-on into the wall.

Ruby fell backward to the ground. This was it.

"Lydia, stab her!" Ally commanded from the floor. At first, Lydia looked stunned. But she nodded bravely and lifted Ruby's smoking sword. She strutted over to Ruby and stabbed her.

"You may have defeated me," Ruby stammered. "But believe me—you won't live much longer…"

With that, Ruby vanished in a puff of red smoke. And not a second later, the sword disappeared from Lydia's hands.

There was a pause. "Is she…dead?" asked Lydia tentatively.

"She *did* say that we've defeated her," Ally replied, picking herself up off the ground and rubbing her broken left arm, which she had landed on when she hit the floor. "But what was that red smoke? Anyway, we'll just assume that she's dead. We have to get out of this room. But first…any sign of Mike and Cyrus yet?"

"Not yet," replied Lydia. "We need a way to find them…"

Lydia began pacing around the room, thinking of a way to find Mike and Cyrus.

Suddenly, she exclaimed, "Oh! Remember last year, we were in this same situation where we couldn't find the boys, then I hacked our wristbands to track theirs?"

"Brilliant!" Ally grinned. Lydia clicked her wristband on, and Ally stood at her shoulder to watch.

Lydia clicked an option that read Texting/Tracking, and a screen with a blue dot and a green dot appeared. The dots were fairly close to each other. Then, a red dot and a yellow dot appeared far away from the blue and the green—Ally and Lydia.

"They're not in this maze; that's for sure," Ally concluded.

"Actually, it's less of a maze and more of a labyrinth," Lydia corrected. "There are no dead ends."

"Well, they're not in this lobyranth thingy or whatever you just said. They must have gone down the Emerald corridor," Ally explained.

"We have to go after them," said Lydia. "I did see a way out just outside of this room."

"Great! Let's go, then!" Ally exclaimed.

And so the two of them left the Ruby Labyrinth and headed for the Emerald hallway.

## CHAPTER FIFTEEN

# Through the Emerald Corridor

ALLY AND LYDIA MADE IT OUT OF THE RUBY LABYRINTH AND KEPT WALKING STRAIGHT TO THE EXIT.

"Have you seen Wiggles anywhere?" Lydia asked. "While we were inside the Labyrinth, we were just walking, and he disappeared!"

"The same thing happened with Aristar," Ally said. "I think Zortavka may have something to do with it. No, I don't think, *I know* Zortavka did it."

"Oh no. I think you're right. That is *not* good. *Not* good at all."

They entered the golden-floored room that led to the three corridors and approached the Emerald corridor.

Suddenly, Ally began to hear something at the end of the passageway. She stopped to listen.

It sounded like someone saying something...no, *shouting* something. It sounded like a girl's voice. Ally had never heard it before, but the more she listened, she realized that it sounded familiar; it sounded like one of the Sirens.

It was Emerald. Ally had thought there would be some sort of challenge to find her, like there had been for Ruby, but apparently there wasn't.

"Ally, do you hear that?" Lydia asked.

"Uh-huh," Ally replied uneasily. "We have to go. Now."

She broke into a run down the rest of the corridor, Lydia following close behind.

Ally couldn't believe what she saw when she stepped into the next room.

Everything was in total chaos. Emerald—who looked completely different from how she had when they first met at school—was hovering in midair, holding a scepter, wildly shooting beams of light—spells, or curses—from the tip of it in every direction.

The entire room seemed to be made of stone, as if it was inside of a mountain. There were gigantic boulders scattered around the huge room.

Emerald continued shouting. "Where did you two young idiots go!? You can run, but you can't hide…!" She paused, looking unsure. "Hmm. I detect more of your kind…" She began to slowly turn in the direction of Ally and Lydia.

Ally grabbed Lydia's wrist, and they ran behind one of the boulders. Ally soon realized that Mike and Cyrus were also behind the boulder, hiding from Emerald.

"Where have you two been?" Lydia gasped.

"We've been here, trying to fight Emerald," Mike gasped, sounding as though he had just finished running a marathon. "But clearly, that's…not going very well."

"We figured we could cover more ground if the two of you fought Ruby, and we fought Emerald," Cyrus explained. "But she's been trying to cast spells on us like crazy, and we haven't been able to really *fight* her yet."

"We don't have very much time before she spots us," said Ally. She looked up, just to see that Emerald had found them. "Actually, we have no time at all. Follow my lead."

Ally bolted out from behind the boulder and into the open. She waved her arms around frantically, yelling, "Come and get me, Emerald!"

"Oh, if it isn't Ally Lancaster," Emerald rasped. "You know, you're very brave. But there's a fine line between bravery and stupidity, and you have officially crossed it, Ally."

"I'm not stupid," Ally said under her breath.

"What was that?"

"I'M NOT STUPID!" Ally shot back. She swiftly pulled out her sword.

Emerald pointed her scepter at Ally and cast a spell. A beam of green light shot out from the tip of it and sped directly at Ally. She dropped to the ground and rolled out of the way, standing up just to see another spell being fired at her. She dropped and rolled again, then got to her feet and ran before Emerald had another chance to turn her into a snail—or whatever the curses did.

"Come down to the ground!" Ally shouted. "It's much nicer down here!"

"Nice try," Emerald smirked. She fired another curse at Ally. Dropping and rolling was hurting her injured arm even more, so she couldn't really do that. She decided on a different strategy, pleading silently for it to work as she pulled out her shield and held it in front of her.

To her surprise, the spell ricocheted off the shield and flew back at Emerald.

Emerald's expression went from smirking to shocked as she was hit by her own curse. She was knocked out of the air, and she landed on the ground clumsily. She quickly got back up, but at least she was no longer floating.

Ally looked at her shield, amazed. *How did that spell just bounce off of it? It would have just flown straight through a regular shield. Maybe it's made of a special material? It's just emerald metal with opal encrusted edges...wait. Emerald metal! It's made of the same material as that scepter! And that means that any spells fired from the scepter will just bounce right off of my shield!*

Pleased with her discovery, Ally held on to her shield, grinning. She had a way to defeat Emerald. Speaking of which...Ally had to focus.

"It *is* nicer down on the ground," Emerald commented sarcastically, glaring over her shoulder at Ally. She whipped around, pointing the scepter at Ally, and fired about ten spells at her at once.

Ally dropped to her knees and whipped her shield around in a quick circle, blocking nine of the ten curses. The last one whizzed past her ear and hit a boulder— which suddenly transformed into a chicken.

*Note to self: DO NOT get hit by one of those spells*, Ally thought as she watched the boulder-chicken wander around in circles. She turned back around, and another curse was shooting straight at her face.

"Whoa!" Ally gasped as she ducked and held her shield above her to block the spell. It bounced off and went flying                    at                    Emerald.

It smacked her in the face, knocking her to the ground. Ally dashed back to her friends, who were still cowering behind a boulder.

"My shield reflects all of her spells," Ally said breathlessly. "It's made of emerald metal, and so is her staff. But I think she's on to me by now. She probably won't fall for it anymore."

"What if we go out there and run around to distract her, while you use your shield to bounce back as many curses as possible?" Mike suggested.

Lydia looked like she could run away screaming at any moment, but she covered her mouth and stayed put. "But then *we* might get hit with the spells and die!"

"Not if you're careful," Ally said firmly. "We have to do it. Let's go."

Ally, Lydia, Mike and Cyrus all ran out from behind the boulder.

"So there are *four* of you?" Emerald said, raising an eyebrow. She rolled her eyes. "Fun."

"On the count of three, scatter," Ally muttered out of the corner of her mouth. "One…two…*three*!"

And so they all scattered around the room, Ally's friends yelling things like "Over here!" or "Come and get me, Emerald!" or, in Lydia's case, "AAAAH!"

Emerald couldn't figure out who to aim her spells at. And when she tried to fire a spell at any of Ally's friends, Ally would swoop in and block them with her shield, causing Emerald to keep getting hit with her own spells. Over time, they wore her down a lot, and this strategy seemed to be working well.

Until things took a turn for the worst.

Emerald was definitely getting tired, but so were Ally, Lydia, Mike and Cyrus. Suddenly, Emerald seemed to have a second wind. Ally and her friends couldn't keep up with her.

Emerald fired a spell at Mike. He was all the way across the room from Ally, so she didn't make it on time.

When the beam of light hit Mike, a bright green lightning bolt struck in that spot, and suddenly, Mike had vanished without a trace.

Lydia gasped loudly. Ally stopped in her tracks.

Ally wasn't paying attention when she heard another bolt of lightning strike. Ally whipped her head in the direction that Cyrus had been standing—he, too, had disappeared.

Ally had no chance to think when a third lightning bolt hit Lydia. She vanished.

"What did you do to my friends?" Ally demanded.

"Oh, let's just say they won't be able to assist you anymore," Emerald replied slyly.

Ally couldn't figure it out completely, but all she knew was that she was responsible for her friends' possible deaths. She had to make up for her mistakes and defeat Emerald.

Emerald positioned her scepter to shoot a curse at Ally. But Ally refused to let the same thing happen to her that had happened to her friends.

Emerald uttered a spell, and a ball of green light came speeding at Ally. She whipped out her shield, and the curse ricocheted off of it. It flew back to Emerald at light speed, smacking her in the face.

The spells didn't have the same effect on Emerald, but she was still knocked off her feet, and this was good enough for Ally to make her move.

She sprinted over to Emerald and snatched the scepter up off the ground.

"Wha—? NO! You can't use that!" Emerald hissed. But Ally ignored her.

The only problem was, she didn't know any spells except for the ones that Camilla Dariva had used—and the ability to conjure a jet ski wouldn't do her much good right now.

But there was one thing that she knew how to do with the scepter—and that was to control objects. Ally had a plan in mind. This had to work.

She pointed the staff at one of the massive boulders in the room. She had never used a scepter before, but the way to use it just sort of came to her.

Her eyes locked on the boulder, and she used the scepter to guide it toward Emerald.

She had to do this—for her friends—for her school—for her mission to defeat all three sirens—this would be the last step in doing so. The 10,000-pound, enormous boulder was halfway between Emerald and where it had started—the boulder was so heavy and hard to move that it was excruciatingly painful—she had to do this—no matter how hard it was—she couldn't—give—IN…

Soon enough, the boulder was on top of Emerald. The boulder disappeared in a cloud of emerald-green smoke, and when the smoke cleared, Ally realized Emerald wasn't there either.

The scepter clattered to the ground and rolled away, and Ally dropped to the ground, panting. Her feelings were mixed:

Happy: All 3 Gemstone Sirens had been defeated.

Shocked: Had she really just done that?

Confused: Was that really it?

Eager: Eager to fight Zortavka at the end of the Dark Gem corridor.

Worried: What had happened to all her friends?

Exhausted: Both from moving that boulder and…when was the last time she had slept?

She decided that she should probably start trying to figure out what Emerald had done to her friends. So after she had a minute to catch her breath, she left the Emerald Corridor and set off toward the golden-floored room.

A great wave of relief washed over Ally as she stepped out of the Emerald corridor to find all three of her friends—and better yet, all four of the pets—waiting in the golden-floored room.

Though, there was something different about them all. For some reason, Lydia, Mike and Cyrus didn't seem to have their weapons. Ally checked to make sure she still had her sword and shield on her—she did. Why didn't her friends?

But what really concerned Ally was that all of the pets were acting like normal animals. Aristar and Biggie were trying to dig a hole in the ground, Wiggles was hopping around aimlessly, and Ediz was stomping in circles. Ally soon realized the reason for this.

Their collars had vanished.

"Ally!" Lydia gasped. She ran over to Ally, followed by Mike, Cyrus, and Aristar. "What happened? Did you beat Emerald?"

Ally told them the whole story.

"Um…what happened to you guys?" Ally questioned after she finished.

"Oh," Lydia replied, her happy expression falling. "Well, Emerald hit us all with the spells, and then we were teleported back here. We lost all of our gear."

"And if that wasn't bad enough," Cyrus added. "The spell makes it so we can't enter any of the three corridors."

"What do you mean?" Ally asked skeptically.

"Whenever we try to go back down the Emerald corridor, this happens," Mike replied. He walked away from the group and tried to enter the Emerald hallway. But there was some kind of invisible force field there that sent him flying backward the instant he touched it. He demonstrated again—the exact same thing happened.

Ally waved her hand through where the invisible barrier had been. Her hand went right through it, as if it were never there.

"So Zortavka made it so I have to fight her alone," Ally realized.                                   "Clever."

"It's a good thing you dodged the spell on time," said Lydia. "Or else *none* of us would be able to go through the Dark Gem corridor."

This was true. If she hadn't dodged Emerald's spell, they would be completely unable to fight Zortavka.

Though, at the same time, Ally wished that she *had* been hit by the curse. The last thing she wanted to do was to have to fight Zortavka alone again.

But it was the last step to completing her mission. Her quest, her school, her friends—they were all depending on her to finish Zortavka off. Ally was the only one capable of doing it. Whether she was alone or not, she *had* to do this.

Ally bravely proceeded down the Dark Gem corridor.

## CHAPTER SIXTEEN

# The Sirens and the Sea Monster

"HELLO AGAIN, ALLY LANCASTER." Ally determinedly set off in a run toward the end of the pitch-black passageway as Zortavka's raspy voice echoed off the walls.

Finally, Ally reached the end of the tunnel, setting foot in a large, dome-shaped room. Zortavka stood in the center of it, surrounded by red smoke, a malicious grin on her scarred face. Her blazing red hair and eyes looked just the same as Ally had remembered them from their showdown in the Enchanted Fortress. The same went for her horns, trident and tail of a devil.

"Well, well, well. We meet again," the Dark Mistress rasped.

"You're going down, Zortavka," Ally barked.

"Is that so?" Zortavka asked calmly. She tossed her head back and cackled maniacally. "Nonsense."

"Hey!" Ally snapped. "Who won the battle in the Enchanted Fortress, again?"

"Nobody, actually," Zortavka replied, stepping up closer to Ally. "If you had truly won, would I be standing here right now?"

"Um…sure," Ally shrugged. "Anyway, you and I both know I won that fight."

Zortavka ignored this. "I suppose you're awaiting another battle. I'll give you what you want. Only this time, you won't be fighting me."

The Dark Mistress snapped her fingers. Suddenly, Ally was being sucked into a red portal. She surged forward, then backward, but then, in the blink of an eye, Ally found herself on a huge pirate ship. Zortavka stood across from her.

"I'll be seeing you…next time. Well, that is, if there *is* a next time. You probably won't make it out of this fight alive!" Zortavka smirked, and then she vanished in a cloud of bright red smoke.

"Hey! Come back here!" Ally demanded. Ally gazed around the pirate ship. "So…what will I be fighting?"

"You'll see," a voice said from high above. Ally looked up at the mast on her left side to see Ruby standing on top of it. Her long hair was sparkling ruby-red, and so was her billowing dress. Her translucent red cape blew in the wind behind her. The blinding glow of her ruby necklace shattered the darkness of the night.

"But…I thought…?" Ally felt she could stare at Ruby for eternity, but that changed when a different voice spoke from the mast to her right.

"We'll give you a battle to remember," Emerald said softly. Her shimmering emerald-green hair was braided, and her long gloves and glittering shoes matched the color. The emerald pendant on her necklace glowed equally as bright as Ruby's.

"That is, if you live to remember it," a third voice added. Ally looked toward the sound and saw Sapphire standing directly across the ship. Her attire was just the same as it had been atop the lighthouse, but her sapphire pendant glowed much brighter.

"Wait, I thought I defeated all of you!" Ally protested.

Sapphire scoffed. "Knocking *a siren* into *the water*? Not your most brilliant idea."

*Darn it,* Ally thought, smacking herself in the face. *That* wasn't *a very good idea.* "But what about the other two?"

"You really thought we would go down that easily?" Ruby grinned. "No way."

For a moment, Ally stared around at the three pendants, glowing brighter than even the stars. Then, abruptly, all three sirens dove into the sea.

Where they had hit the water, there was a glow. Above that spot, storm clouds began to swirl. Ally positioned her hand on the hilt of her sword, preparing to take action as the glow in the water grew brighter and brighter by the second. The swirling storm clouds grew bigger and darker, and lightning struck the water.

After a minute, Ally tentatively walked over to the edge of the ship to check it out, pulling out her sword slowly as she walked. The glow in the water was blinding. Then, where the light was, the water began to ripple.

And then, an enormous sea serpent emerged from the ocean, splashing water over everything within about a mile. Its gargantuan body was sparkling sapphire blue, and its fins shimmered ruby red and emerald green. Its eyes were bright red and very menacing, and its fangs looked like they could pierce diamond. Embedded in the serpent's forehead were three glittering gems: a sapphire, a ruby and an emerald.

Time froze as Ally gaped at what the Gemstone Sirens had become: a Gemstone Leviathan.

*I need a way to defeat this thing,* Ally thought to herself. *But I don't have very much time right now. I'm definitely wasting time. I HAVE TO STOP DOING THAT. So I guess I'll just...think of something when I can? That is, if I ever can...*

Everything unpaused and the battle began. It started storming, and the waters became rough. The pirate ship rocked violently.

Ally pulled out her sword. It was difficult to see through the pouring rain, and to make matters worse, it was very dark out.

The leviathan made to bite Ally in half. She dove to the ground and rolled out of the way. The monster chomped a giant hole in the wood where Ally had been standing.

The boat abruptly jerked to the side, sending Ally flying into the side of the boat. She slammed into the wall. This was *not* looking good.

Ally got to her feet as fast as possible. The monster was out of reach from her—she couldn't possibly do it any damage, because it was in the water. She *had* to think of a way to beat this thing; if she didn't think fast, she would surely become leviathan food. She had come *much* too far for that to happen.

Ally looked around. Way off in the distance, she spotted Gelesca Cove; the giant cliff, the wrecked shack atop it, and, standing by the cliff, the pets. They seemed to have their collars back, somehow.

The pets could definitely be useful. *Maybe I can fly Aristar to get up closer to the leviathan, and then I'll be able to fight better than from on the ground?* Ally thought. *It's definitely risky, but what other plan do I have? It'll have to work.*

"Aristar!" Ally shouted as loudly as possible. On the faraway island, Aristar turned in her direction and cocked his head to the side, listening. "Come here, quick!"

Aristar got a running start and then took to the skies. He soared through the heavy storm smoothly and landed on the ship right beside Ally. He looked like a soggy black mop in the rain, as always. He acted like the gargantuan sea monster wasn't licking its lips and eyeing them sinisterly–his full attention was on Ally.

Ally quickly mounted Aristar, her sword in hand. They flew upward toward the leviathan's face. It launched at them, and its fangs narrowly missed Aristar's wing.

"Watch out," Ally warned Aristar as the Leviathan took another dive at them. It barely missed.

As Aristar flew in circles around the sea monster, keeping it busy, Ally thought of a plan. *Every monster has a weak spot,* she thought determinedly. *If I could just figure out this one's...*

She scanned over the monster, searching for a weak spot. The gems on its forehead looked promising, that is, *if* Ally and Aristar could get close enough without being shredded into pieces. It was worth a shot; what other plan did they have?

But Zortavka would never make it that easy for her. There had to be something more to breaking the gems— simply stabbing them all wouldn't do. *Think,* Ally urged herself. There was a ruby, an emerald, and a sapphire… they represented each of the Sirens. Maybe, in order to destroy them, she had to break them in the same way that she had (temporarily) defeated each of the sirens individually–stab the ruby with her sword…hit the emerald with a boulder…do something related to lighthouses to the sapphire.

*Perfect,* Ally thought. She brushed the rain-soaked tangles of hair out of her eyes and commanded, "Aristar, take me to the ruby." Obediently, Aristar swooped down at the Leviathan's head. As they flew by, Ally stabbed the ruby with her sword, and she was showered with shards of the shattered gem. They got out of the way just in time for the monster to throw its head back and let out an ear-piercing                                                                            shriek.

Now its full attention was on Ally and Aristar, who were hovering high above its head. With its eyes locked on them, it refused to look away.

"Aristar, can I have a rock?" Ally ordered out the corner of her mouth. A tray slid out from the black lab's collar. On it was a small, smooth stone.

"This will work." Ally tossed the stone into the air, and caught it again. "Aristar, take me to the emerald."

Aristar dove down again, aiming for the emerald this time. But the leviathan's fang snagged his wing. He began to swerve to the side, and Ally slipped off of his back.

And if she wasn't wet enough already, she took a plunge into the stormy sea. She opened her eyes underwater and looked around for the ladder back on to the pirate ship.

Ally nearly shot like a missile out of the water when she turned to see the leviathan's bloodshot eyes staring at her.

Then, the sea monster barreled directly at her, mouth open wide. Ally swam out of the way just on time, and an idea came to her at that very moment. She wrapped her arms around the serpent's neck as it went by, and it crashed through the surface of the water with her clinging to its neck.

She climbed up to the monster's head. It jerked its head around violently, trying to shake her off, but Ally refused to let go. She pulled out the small stone and struck the emerald with it multiple times before the shimmering gem shattered.

Finally, she let go and slipped off the leviathan's head. Aristar caught her, and they began soaring around the monster again.

*Just one gem left to go!* Ally thought, and for the first time, she felt a glimmer of hope. She might actually defeat the leviathan. She might actually return to Willow Reins. This whole mission might finally end...

But that quickly changed.

As they were flying by, Ally wasn't paying attention to the leviathan. She was too busy being happy that they might win this fight.

The leviathan took this opportunity to sink its fangs into Ally's leg.

Ally suddenly felt a searing pain in her leg. Instantly, she knew; she had been bitten.

White-hot pain was spreading throughout her leg, and Ally began to feel drowsy—the leviathan's venom had the same effects of the siren song. This *couldn't* happen. Not when they were this close. No way.

Ally lost control of Aristar and they swerved to the side. Too dizzy to stay balanced, Ally slid off Aristar's back and hit the ground of the pirate ship with a *thud*.

The world spun like a globe, and different features of the pirate ship blurred together. *This is it,* Ally thought. *We have no chance now.*

But a different thought crossed her mind: This *couldn't* be the end. Ally wouldn't let it be. She wouldn't go down like this.

She stood up clumsily and mounted Aristar, trying to ignore the throbbing pain in her leg. Aristar took off, and they flew over the Leviathan's head. Even through the intense storm, the darkness of the night and the dizziness, Ally held on with every ounce of strength she had left.

Aristar dove at the Leviathan's head. The wind rushed past Ally's ears and her hair blew behind her. Her ears were ringing, and she couldn't think straight.

But she needed a way to destroy the sapphire that related somehow to the lighthouse. The only thing she could think of was using a light from Aristar's collar, shining it in the monster's eyes and striking the sapphire while it was blinded.

"Aristar… light," Ally managed. A bright light shone from the front of Aristar's collar, and he pointed it at the leviathan's eyes. The monster was blinded  but only for a few seconds.

Ally raised her sword. This was her final chance.

She stabbed the sapphire, hard. The leviathan let out a shrill shriek, and the life drained from its eyes. Red, blue and green smoke surrounded the sea monster as it formed into a large sphere of glowing light.

Aristar landed on the ship. The world was a giant blur to Ally. Things slowly started to go dark. The Gemstone Leviathan had been defeated, and that was amazing, but Ally wasn't certain that she would make it off this pirate ship alive.

She was awake just long enough to see the sphere of light explode into the night sky like a firework before she collapsed.

## CHAPTER SEVENTEEN

# The Gemstone Sirens

"Wait. Is that…Ally Lancaster?"

"Yes, it has to be."

"Is she…dead?"

"I hope so."

"Seriously??"

"I'm kidding! Mostly."

Ally woke up lying on the damp wooden ground of the pirate ship, staring up at the cloudless morning sky. The sound of distant conversation drifted to her ears. What was going on?

She sat up. Standing across from her was Aristar, along with 3 familiar-looking girls. It took Ally a second to register who they really were: Mokona Ami, Camilla Dariva, and Aryanna Parks.

"Um…what's going on?" Ally asked.

"Well, don't be alarmed," Mokona said tentatively. "But *we* were the Gemstone Sirens."

"Wait. You're telling me that *you three* were Ruby, Sapphire, and Emerald, the ones who tried to kill me?" Ally laughed. "Very funny."

But Mokona, Camilla and Aryanna remained dead serious.

"This is probably all so confusing to you, so allow me to explain," said Camilla. "Zortavka kidnapped us all after you encountered us each individually—so, for me, right after you left Kalomono Sands, Zortavka appeared. She demanded that I work for her in disguise, or else she would kill me. So, she put a spell on me that transformed me into Emerald. The same happened to Mokona after you departed from Port Zyleria—she was transformed into Sapphire—and Aryanna, after your run-in with each other back at school—she became Ruby."

"So, you were possessed," Ally said.

"Exactly," said Mokona. "It was a horrible experience. It was like sharing a mind with Zortavka…not being able to think or move for yourself, being forced to do things against your will…"

"I kind of liked working with Zortavka," Aryanna interjected. Both Mokona and Camilla shot her angry looks, and she shrugged. "What? I liked fighting against Ally."

None of it made sense, but at the same time, everything made sense. On top of the lighthouse, Ally had recognized Sapphire, but hadn't been able to figure out who she was. When she had left Kalomono Sands, Camilla had vanished in a puff of *emerald-green* smoke. During the battle with Emerald, Emerald had been using a scepter— one that resembled Camilla's. Ever since Ally and Aryanna had run into each other back at school, she had been absent from classes. She hadn't recognized her during the fight because Ally avoided Aryanna as much as possible at school, and they didn't spend nearly enough time with each other for Ally to be able to recognize her in disguise.

But still, some things didn't quite add up. Mokona, Camilla and Aryanna, as themselves, had existed at the same time as the Sirens. Ally had met the Sirens at school, and later met the three of them—as themselves.

"I know what you're thinking," said Mokona. "Originally, Zortavka had used three of her own dark servants to play the roles of the Gemstone Sirens."

"But remember when she hacked into your dog's collar last year?" Camilla chimed in. "She programmed a tracking device into it, and so she's been able to track you ever since. After you talked to Aryanna at school, she assumed that you were friends with her—"

"Even though we're definitely *not*," Aryanna cut in.

"Right," said Camilla. "She came up with the brilliant idea to make you fight people you were 'friends' with. So, she kidnapped Aryanna and swapped her servant out with her to play Ruby. She did the same with me, after you stopped and talked with me at Kalomono Sands, and she already knew you were friends with Mokona after the Enchanted Fortress adventure."

"But why not kidnap my actual friends and turn them against me?" Ally asked.

"She knew you'd recognize them all immediately," Mokona replied. "It was all part of Zortavka's masterful plan to kill you."

"Wow," said Ally, processing all of this new information. "Also, I thought I defeated each of you individually. How were all three of you still alive after that?"

"Zortavka teleported us each back to her the instant you defeated us," explained Camilla. "She healed all of us with magic. Oh, and speaking of healing with magic, I healed your leg for you. It's still in the mending process, though, so just be careful."

Ally hadn't even realized; her leg, which was now wrapped in a thick layer of bandages, didn't hurt anymore.

"Thanks," she said.

"Don't mention it," Camilla chirped. "Besides…how could I ever repay you for trying to kill you and your friends?"

"That wasn't you. That was Zortavka," said Ally, standing up. Her leg hurt a little, but not even close to how much it did when it was first bitten. She was able to walk just fine. "But speaking of friends…I should meet up with my friends back on Gelesca Cove. And you three are coming with me."

"Ugh. Come on! I don't want to go with you," Aryanna huffed stubbornly, checking her pink-painted nails. "I'll just swim back to Willow Reins."

Ally groaned. "Look, I'm not happy about it either, but I don't think Principal Washiarota would be very happy with me if I told him I abandoned you on Gelesca Cove just because I don't like you."

"Fine," Aryanna scoffed. "But don't expect me to be happy about it."

"I liked you better when you were Ruby," Ally muttered under her breath.

Aryanna opened her mouth to protest, but Mokona cut in. "Your fighting isn't helping. We have to pick up your friends at Gelesca Cove and then get back to school. And we have to do it fast; the farewell party is starting in an hour."

Mokona meant what she said about them having to go fast. The school year would be over soon…

# CHAPTER EIGHTEEN

# The Quest's End

WHILE CAMILLA USED HER MAGICAL SCEPTER TO GUIDE THE WRECKED PIRATE SHIP BACK TO THE SANDY SHORE OF GELESCA COVE, ALLY WRAPPED ARISTAR'S TORN WING WITH BANDAGES AND ARYANNA COMPLAINED ABOUT HAVING TO RETURN TO WILLOW REINS WITH ALLY.

"Just leave me here," she moaned.

"Just shut your mouth and try not to be so dramatic!" Ally hissed. Once she finished repairing Aristar's wing, she looked around the ship. A small glowing object lying on the ground caught her eye. Curious, she walked over to check it out.

It turned out to be not one, but three objects: a ruby, a sapphire and an emerald—the pendants from the Sirens' necklaces. *I'll hold on to these,* Ally thought as she snatched the gems up off the ground.

Once the boat docked on Gelesca Cove, Ally was the first to jump off the pirate ship. Lydia, Mike and Cyrus were waiting on the shore with their pets, and Ally was relieved to see that all of their weapons and gear had been returned to them.

"Oh my gosh, Ally!" Lydia exclaimed. "And…Mokona, Camilla and *Aryanna*??"

"Yeah, about that…" Ally laughed. She told them the whole story, from crossing paths with Zortavka to the battle with the Leviathan to who the Gemstone Sirens really were.

"So let me get this straight," said Cyrus. "*You three* were the Gemstone Sirens?"

Mokona nodded. "But don't worry—we're not evil anymore."

Ally glanced down at her wristband. There was a new announcement from the principal, which included a countdown to the end of the year.

*The school year ends in...*
*0 days, 0 hours, 7 minutes, and 14 seconds*
*Report to the cafeteria for the farewell party within an hour.*

"We have to get back to Willow Reins," said Ally urgently. "And *fast*. We should get going *ASAP*."

"I should be returning to the Dariva Fortress; my brother is probably wondering where I've been for so long," Camilla stated. "But also, you won't make it back to Willow Reins on time if you're traveling via dueling pet."

"Then how are we supposed to get back?" Ally asked.

"I'll teleport you there, of course," Camilla chirped. She pulled out her ruby-tipped scepter and pointed it towards the rest of the group. "Hold on to your hats—*Requatica!*"

There was a blinding flash of green, and Ally found herself standing on the wide brick walkway that led to the entrance of Willow Reins. But the instant she arrived, she was knocked off her feet by someone pushing past her. She landed with a *thud* on the brick walkway, and then she was nearly run over by what she soon realized was a huge crowd of students and pets pouring out of the wide-open school doors.

Ally's friends helped her up, and they all fled to the side of the walkway to avoid the huge rush of students.

"Come on, we missed the farewell party!" Ally groaned.

"But there's still time to run inside, pack our belongings, and say hello to Principal Washiarota," said Mokona.

"Ok, Let's go then!" Mike exclaimed. The five of them—minus Aryanna, who had abandoned them the second they had arrived—dashed into the cafeteria, closely followed by their pets.

Principal Washiarota was still at the podium at the head of the cafeteria where he had been standing for his end-of-the-year speech, discussing something with Sir Rewndo. They both turned their heads at the sound of Ally and her friends entering the room.

"Ah, I don't believe it!" Washiarota exclaimed. "Miss Lancaster, Miss Whysperia, Mister Sticio and Mister

Lavacis have returned at long last! Oh, and even Miss Ami as well? It truly is a miracle!"

"A'y!" Sir Rewndo yelled in delight. "Wh're 'ave ya been?"

Ally thought about the whole adventure, debating what parts to tell and which not to. There was the ride on The Rovast, the Triacontapus attack, Ally's visits to both Kalomono Sands and Port Zyleria, the epic battle with Sapphire atop the lighthouse, fighting the Electrowolves, the battles with Ruby and Emerald, crossing paths with Zortavka, fighting the Leviathan, and finding out who the Gemstone Sirens really were.

Ally could have described all of that, but instead she replied, "It's…a long story."

"Is that so?" asked Washiarota. "Very well, then. You five should go and pack your belongings quickly; your families are already here to pick you up."

So Ally, Lydia, Aristar and Wiggles went to their dorm room for the final time that year, and Ally packed up her belongings. There wasn't very much to pack; mainly just her sword, shield, and the gemstone-pendant necklaces that had once belonged to the Gemstone Sirens. She packed those as a souvenir from this year's adventure.

Before long, Ally found herself walking out the doors of Willow Reins, saying goodbye to her friends.

"See you guys next year!" Ally called to her friends as she and Aristar broke off from the group and ran to her parents' van.

"You're late," Ari said. "And where have you *been* all year?"

"Uh…nowhere special," Ally grinned.

During the car ride home, Ally told her family the story over and over again, in hopes that they might believe it at least a little bit.

But every time, as expected, her parents responded with nothing but a chuckle. "You have quite the imagination," they would say.

Ally began counting down the days until the next school year started the minute she got home. Even though this was the second year in which she had almost died fighting monsters, there was still no question that she would be back next year.

And she couldn't wait.

A new message from my Dueling Dog, Sam:

5tt4/≥;.÷.li9kjiuy6tgfxz  pizza

}]98[7cxz0o09 bj
£†¢
xgdzfcsdafzfdzsxfdsazxszsdferfzxcfvfzdszddzxcgvbdfsz
cxfgv bcygt" ojka9uiktyi678iuythj4gref3dsa QAZSWW

He actually typed this!!

# Acknowledgements

**Special Thanks:**

Thanks to Mom and Dad, for taking time out of your busy schedules to help edit this book. Thanks to Grandpa and Grandpa, for always encouraging me to keep writing. Thanks to all my family, friends, and pets, including Sam, Arlo, Bartlet and Snoopy, plus Simon and Celeste, the best cats in the world.

**Final Manuscript Line and Copy Edits**: Jessica Smithers, Jason Smithers

**Cover Art**: Jason Smithers

**Cover Design and Type**: Amanda Tuttle

# ABOUT THE AUTHOR

Maci is a four-time author. At the age of eight, she told her parents that she wanted to write and illustrate a book. Her parents explained to her that if she did every single part of the process (storyboarding, writing, illustrating, page layout, choosing fonts, etc.), then they would guide her through self-publishing. She finished the process in 3-4 months with her first picture book titled *Maci and Addie's Fairy Adventure,* followed by her second picture book *The Portal.*

In the midst of the challenging year that was 2020, when most kids were faced with adversity, ten-year-old Maci harnessed her creative spirit to complete the initial installment of the series, titled *Ally Lancaster & The Enchanted Fortress,* marking her third literary endeavor and her inaugural novella. Two years later, at the age of 12, 2022, she completed this sequel, *Ally Lancaster & The Gemstone Sirens.*

178